IN MEDIAS RES

What Reviewers Say About Bold Strokes Books

"With its expected unexpected twists, vivid characters and healthy dose of humor, *Blind Curves* is a very fun read that will keep you guessing."—*Bay Windows*

"In a succinct film style narrative, with scenes that move, a character-driven plot, and crisp dialogue worthy of a screenplay...the Richfield and Rivers novels are...an engaging Hollywood mystery...series."—*Midwest Book Review*

Force of Nature "...is filled with nonstop, fast paced action. Tornadoes, raging fire blazes, heroic and daring rescues...Baldwin does a fine job of describing the fast-paced scenes and inspiring the reader to keep on turning the pages."—*L-word.com Literature*

In the Jude Devine mystery series the "...characters seem fully capable of walking away from the particulars of whodunit and engaging the reader in other aspects of their lives."—*Lambda Book Report*

Mine "...weaves a tale of yearning, love, lust, and conflict resolution...a believable plot, with strong characters in a charming setting." – *Just About Write*

"While these two women struggle with their issues, there is some very, very hot sex. If you enjoy complex characters and passionate sex scenes, you'll love *Wild Abandon*."—*MegaScene*

"*Course of Action* is a romance...populated with a host of captivating and amiable characters. The glimpses into the lifestyles of the rich and beautiful people are rather like guilty pleasures...a most satisfying and entertaining reading experience."—*Midwest Book Review*

The Clinic is "...a spellbinding novel."—*Just About Write*

"*Unexpected Sparks* lived up to its promise and was thoroughly enjoyable...Dartt did a lovely job at building the relationship between Kate and Nikki."—*Lambda Book Report*

"*Sequestered Hearts*...is everything a romance should be. It is teeming with longing, heartbreak, and of course, love. As pure romances go, it is one of the best in print today."—*L-word.com Literature*

"*The Exile and the Sorcerer* is a mesmerizing read, a tour-de-force packed with adventure, ordeals, complex twists and turns, and the internal introspection of appealing characters."—*Midwest Book Review*

The Spanish Pearl is "...both science fiction and romance in this adventurous tale...A most entertaining read, with a sequel already in the works. Hot, hot, hot!"—*Minnesota Literature*

"A deliciously sexy thriller...*Dark Valentine* is funny, scary, and very realistic. The story is tightly written and keeps the reader gripped to the exciting end."—*Just About Write*

"*Punk Like Me*...is different. It is engaging. It is life-affirming. Frankly, it is genius. This is a rare book in that it has a soul; one that is laid bare for all to see."—*Just About Write*

"*Chance* is not a novel about the music industry; it is about a woman discovering herself as she muddles through all the trappings of fame."—*Midwest Book Review*

Sweet Creek "...is sublimely in tune with the times."—*Q-Syndicate*

"*Forever Found*...neatly combines hot sex scenes, humor, engaging characters, and an exciting story."—*MegaScene*

Shield of Justice is a "...well-plotted...lovely romance...I couldn't turn the pages fast enough!"—Ann Bannon, author of *The Beebo Brinker Chronicles*

The 100th Generation is "...filled with ancient myths, Egyptian gods and goddesses, legends, and, most wonderfully, it contains the lesbian equivalent of Indiana Jones living and working in modern Egypt."—*Just About Write*

Sword of the Guardian is "...a terrific adventure, coming of age story, a romance, and tale of courtly intrigue, attempted assassination, and gender confusion...a rollicking fun book and a must-read for those who enjoy courtly light fantasy in a medieval-seeming time."—*Midwest Book Review*

"*Of Drag Kings and the Wheel of Fate*'s lush rush of a romance incorporates reincarnation, a grounded transman and his peppy daughter, and the dark moods of a troubled witch—wonderful homage to Leslie Feinberg's classic gender-bending novel, *Stone Butch Blues*."—*Q-Syndicate*

In *Running with the Wind* "...the discussions of the nature of sex, love, power, and sexuality are insightful and represent a welcome voice from the view of late-20-something characters today."—*Midwest Book Review*

"Rich in character portrayal, *The Devil Inside* is an unusual, unpredictable, and thought-provoking love story that will have the reader questioning the definition of right and wrong long after she finishes the book."—*Just About Write*

Wall of Silence "...is perfectly plotted and has a very real voice and consistently accurate tone, which is not always the case with lesbian mysteries."—*Midwest Book Review*

IN MEDIAS RES

by

Yolanda Wallace

2010

IN MEDIAS RES
© 2010 By Yolanda Wallace. All Rights Reserved.

ISBN 10: 1-60282-142-9
ISBN 13: 978-1-60282-142-2

This Trade Paperback Original Is Published By
Bold Strokes Books, Inc.
P.O. Box 249
Valley Falls, NY 12185

First Edition: March 2010

This is a work of fiction. Names, characters, places, and incidents are the product of the author's imagination or are used fictitiously. Any resemblance to actual persons, living or dead, business establishments, events, or locales is entirely coincidental.

This book, or parts thereof, may not be reproduced in any form without permission.

Credits
Editor: Cindy Cresap
Production Design: Stacia Seaman
Cover Design By Sheri (graphicartist2020@hotmail.com)

Acknowledgments

A wise woman once told me that a writer should be a person on whom nothing is lost. With that in mind, I am fully aware of the tremendous opportunity I have been afforded by Bold Strokes Books to make my dream of becoming a writer a reality. Thank you to Radclyffe and the Bold Strokes family for making my dreams come true. Thank you also to my patient partner, who loves me even when I'm suffering through the throes of writer's block.

Dedication

To Dita.
Thank you for choosing me.

In medias res is Latin for "into the middle of things." It usually describes a narrative that begins, not at the beginning of a story, but somewhere in the middle—usually at some crucial point in the action. The term comes from the ancient Roman poet Horace, who advised the aspiring epic poet to go straight to the heart of the story instead of commencing at the beginning.

—Jack Lynch, *Glossary of Literary and Rhetorical Terms*, 1999.
http://andromeda.rutgers.edu/~jlynch/Terms/inmediasres.html
(accessed December 2009).

CHAPTER ONE

I was in the middle of the airport when it happened.

I was running as fast as I could, dodging one startled person after another, when I realized I didn't know where I was running or why. I couldn't even remember my own name. I know it sounds clichéd—like the opening lines of a bad film noir—but it was true.

I hazarded a glance over my left shoulder to make sure no one was chasing me. When I turned around, I nearly collided with an elderly woman pulling a rolling carry-on bag behind her. The bag—Louis Vuitton or a very good knockoff—was bigger than she was. She brushed my cooties off her crisp linen suit and muttered something I couldn't hear. Biting back a more colorful response, I apologized to her, then stepped aside to catch my breath. With my heart pounding the way it was, that wasn't easy.

My first reaction was abject panic. It's one thing not to know where you are. To not know *who* you are? That's something else altogether.

Standing with my hands on my knees, I sucked air into my burning lungs. I looked like a track athlete after an especially grueling race. Only I didn't have a medal to show for it.

A couple of people looked at me with concern on their

faces as they passed by me. Most kept walking as if they had seen it all before. No one stopped and, more importantly, no one seemed to recognize me.

Security personnel wandered the concourse, but I couldn't bring myself to ask any of them for help. I felt vaguely ashamed. As if what was happening to me—or had already happened—was somehow my fault.

My mind raced as fast as my heart beat. I had signs to tell me where I was—*Welcome to O'Hare*, they blared—but I had nothing to tell me who I was. Or did I?

In my left hand was a ticket to Key West. Coach, with a connecting flight in Miami. I was on my way to Florida and I wasn't rolling in dough. Two things I could now be sure of.

I dove headfirst into the steady flow of foot traffic, allowing myself to drift with the current until it led me to the nearest board that displayed the list of departing and arriving flights. The flight that corresponded to the ticket in my hand was taking off in ten minutes. That explained why I had been running. Another mystery solved.

I was standing in gate seventeen. The one I needed was fourteen gates away. After shifting into top speed again, I made it to the gate just as the attendants were preparing to close the doors. I thrust my ticket toward the nearest attendant, who flashed me an irritated smile.

"We've been paging you all over the airport," she said as she ran my ticket through the scanner. "Running a little late, are we, Mrs. Stanton?"

"That's the least of my problems."

Through the window, I could see the ground crew deicing the plane. I wanted to be out there with them. I needed a nice blast of cold air to cool me down—and to dry the semicircular sweat stains that darkened my T-shirt.

I was dressed in layers—a long-sleeved compression shirt

under a Rolling Stones concert T-shirt topped off by a wool peacoat. My jeans weren't lined, but my boots certainly were. I could feel the faux fur rubbing against my wool socks.

Stress, embarrassment, and my mad dash from whatever had been my starting point combined to ratchet my body temperature up a good ten degrees. I pulled off my coat and draped it over my left arm. I used the other arm to wipe perspiration off my forehead.

The attendants, crisp and cool in their airline-issue uniforms, looked like they wanted nothing to do with me. I couldn't blame them. God knows how I must have looked. The window behind them didn't act as a very good mirror. In it, I could see a faint reflection of myself. I was tall and angular with shoulder-length blond hair and haunted brown eyes. I wasn't covered in blood and I wasn't in pain, so whatever trauma I had experienced to deprive me of my memory must have been mental instead of physical.

I was filled with questions, but I didn't know where to find any of the answers. Were they in Miami, Key West, or Chicago? What did I have to lose?

I had come to the airport for a reason and that reason was obviously to go to Florida, so I kept going in that direction.

I retrieved my boarding pass then headed down the corridor and stepped onto the waiting plane.

"Welcome aboard," one of the flight attendants chirped. I mumbled a thank you and began making my way to the back of the aircraft. The other passengers threw daggers at me with their eyes as if the flight crew had held up the flight for me. The proud owner of a seat in the tail section, I doubted I was that important.

I collapsed into my seat and quickly fastened my seat belt. I wanted to get settled in so I could examine the contents of the backpack slung over my left shoulder.

A black leather clutch inside the main compartment of the backpack housed $500 in cash, a driver's license, a couple of gold credit cards, a debit card, a medical insurance card, and what I guessed were family photos. A checkbook register indicated I had just shy of $14,000 in the bank, supplemented monthly by $6,000 deposits noted in the register as "allowance." Nice work if you could get it.

The driver's license was issued by the state of Illinois on July 16, 2007, and was due for renewal on August 24, 2011. The accompanying photo looked more like a mug shot, but I was more interested in the information the tiny piece of plastic imparted than in whether the picture was a good likeness of me.

According to my license, my name was Sydney P. Stanton. I lived on Waveland Avenue. I was five foot eleven, weighed one hundred and thirty-five pounds, and I was an organ donor. That last part was good to know. I was in desperate need of a brain transplant. The one I had wasn't working. Sputtering along, it hadn't shut down completely. I still knew with relative certainty that two plus two equaled four, but processing more complex thoughts took a concerted effort. It felt a bit like walking through mud. I got where I was going, but it took me a while to get there. And I got awful dirty on the way.

The passenger across the aisle from me was reading what I assumed was a current copy of the *Chicago Tribune*. The headline on the front page announced "Subway Slasher Gets 10 Years." I looked at the date above the forty-eight point type. January 12, 2010. I compared the date on the newspaper to the one listed on my license as my date of birth. In seven months, I would be thirty-two years old.

"Too young to be senile, but old enough to know better."

The phrase popped into my head unbidden. The voice reciting it was a woman's voice, but it wasn't my voice. My mother's, perhaps? My grandmother's? Was I remembering something from my past, my present, or was I going crazy on top of everything else?

I sifted through the photos in the wallet, hoping that one would strike a chord in me and my memory would come rushing back completely instead of a fragment here or there. Then again, if seeing my own face couldn't bring me around, how could I expect it from someone else's?

The first photo was a twenty-year-old picture of my parents, my brother, and me. I knew not because I remembered but because of what was written on the back. "The Paulsens— Sidney, Patricia, Sydney, and Patrick—December 1990." The four of us were decked out in festive Christmas sweaters in front of a roaring fire. The fire was obviously fake, but our smiles seemed genuine.

Brown-haired with a soft chin and round body, my brother looked like my mother; I looked like my father. I guess that explained the names.

I stared at the smiling faces, willing myself to make a connection with one or all of them. For all the kinship I felt for the strangers staring back at me, the photo could have been nothing more than a pre-packaged insert that had come with the wallet.

The second photo was of me and a woman who looked enough like me to be my sister. The back of the picture, however, revealed she was something else. "Jennifer and Sydney, best friends for life," the handwritten caption proclaimed.

The photo was undated. It looked fairly recent but not new. In it, Jennifer and I wore matching uniforms. Our arms around each other's shoulders, our index fingers in the air, we were apparently attending or participating in some kind of sporting event. Basketball? Soccer? Softball? The picture was cropped too tightly for me to tell what sport we were dressed for. Our upraised arms prevented me from seeing the name of the team we were so proud of. I could make out a patch of green in the background but, unable to see the lines, I couldn't tell for what sport the field of play was marked.

In addition to being "best friends for life," were Jennifer and I sports fans, former teammates, or both? The way I was sucking wind in the airport, whatever athletic career I might have had was a distant memory. In more ways than one.

Then something occurred to me.

I flipped back to the first photo. The one of me and my family. The name on the back of the picture was different from the one on my driver's license. At twelve, I had been Sydney Paulsen. Nineteen years later, I had become Sydney Stanton. That meant I was married. There on the ring finger of my left hand was the proof—a diamond wedding ring and a matching platinum band. How had I not noticed them before?

I stared at the rings for a long moment but couldn't force myself to feel like they were a part of me, no matter how deep the indentations they had made in my skin.

I searched the wallet for photos of my missing husband.

Behind another family portrait, one even older than the previous—I was an infant in this one; my brother looked to be about two or three—was a snapshot of me and a handsome man with black hair and shining green eyes. The picture was taken on or for our wedding day. I was wearing a stunning strapless white gown with a mile-long train. He was resplendent in a dark gray tuxedo. Standing next to a four-tier cake, we each held a glass of champagne. Our arms were entwined as we leaned in close to take a sip of the sparkling drink.

I pulled the picture out of its plastic cover so I could read the back. "Dr. and Mrs. Jack Stanton, 6-12-08."

I flipped the photo over. I was a doctor's wife, the envy of single women everywhere. I had been married to the man in the picture for nineteen months. Though I had obviously loved him at one time—loved him enough to commit my body and my life to him—I felt nothing for him now. Shouldn't the love of my life, if that's what he was, prompt at least a glimmer of recognition?

Where was he? Did he know where I was? Did he even care? What about the rest of my family? Were they tearing their hair out looking for me or were they going about their daily lives blissfully unaware that something was very, very wrong with me?

There was a cell phone in the side pocket of the backpack, but it was of no use to me. As the plane taxied down the runway, the flight attendant who had welcomed me aboard had announced that the use of cell phones was prohibited during the duration of the flight. I would have to wait until the plane landed in Miami before I could scroll through the phone's menu and search the entries in the directory.

I was supposed to touch down in Key West at four thirty-five p.m. Eastern. I glanced at my left wrist, where a silver Citizen silently kept track of the time. It was only ten thirty a.m. Central. With another five hours to kill, I continued searching through the backpack.

The fact that I was headed to Key West was firmly established. What was uncertain was my reason for going there. Was I on vacation? Abandoning six feet of snow and negative wind chills for eighty-degree temperatures seemed like a good idea. Was I meeting someone? If so, who? And why weren't we flying together? Where would I stay? A five-star hotel? Too ritzy for the way I was dressed. A roach motel? Too college road trip for someone who had reached the dark side of thirty. Perhaps something in between.

Behind a bag of toiletries was a leather-bound day planner. With the year only twelve days old, the book wasn't much help. Aside from daily entries at ten a.m. for "gym" and entries on Tuesdays and Thursdays at noon for "spa treatment," there were precious few additional notes.

On January 1 was "watch bowl games with Team Paulsen." That had been an all-day affair.

January 4 had seen me running all over town. At eleven a.m. was "get oil changed." At one p.m. was "meet Mom for lunch at Bob Chinn's." At two thirty was "dentist appt." At four was "p/u dry cleaning—d/o Jack's tux." (I translated the shorthand as "pick up" and "drop off.") At five was "committee meeting @ Gale's—make sure members stick to agenda or it will turn into a sleepover!!" A squiggly line was drawn from seven thirty to nine. Next to it was written, "call out for dinner—Chinese or Thai?"

The next three days had been relatively quiet, with only one entry on January 7: "pick up steaks for party—marinate overnight." There were four entries on January 8, however. At nine thirty a.m. was "p/u Jack's tux." At five was "get to Athena's early for last-minute inspection." From six to eight was "Jen's party." And from eight until one a.m., a five-hour block of time had been carved out for "welcome back Rekowski."

The sole entry on January 9 was at eight p.m.: "dinner w/ Jack at Ambria—talk to him!!" The word "talk" was underlined four times. Underscored with such force that the pen had bitten into the page. That was the last entry until June 12, which was marked with a tentative "anniversary in Paris?"

With no mention of work, I had no idea what I did for a living—if anything. My monthly allowance seemed generous enough to cover all my expenses—the gym membership and trips to the spa, among other frivolous things. My schedule made me sound like a glorified errand girl. Perhaps being a doctor's wife was my only identity. With the constant trips to the body shop for toning and buffing, I apparently worked hard to maintain that identity.

Had the pressure to remain perfect gotten to be too much?

The address book in the back of the day planner contained a string of names with complete contact information for each—snail and e-mail addresses, accompanied by home, work, and cell phone numbers. Apparently, I was Miss Popular.

I flipped to the back of the address book. Muscle memory directed me to the *V* tab. I slid my finger down the lined page. Under the entry for Vacation House was an address on United Street in Key West, Florida.

Aside from a tube of ChapStick and an unopened pack of Trident, my pockets were empty. I searched the backpack for a set of keys. I found them stowed in a side pocket next to the one that held the cell phone. I slipped the keys into the front pocket of my jeans. I felt more secure having them near me.

I had figured out my destination, thanks to some Sherlock Holmes–style deduction, but the reason for my trip still eluded me. Not quite as elementary, my dear Watson.

I turned back to the entry for January 9. The one for dinner with Jack at Ambria. The "talk to him" concerned me, as did the deeply etched lines under the word. Had I talked to him and the conversation had ended badly? If that were the case, why hadn't I scratched out the June entry for anniversary in Paris? And why had I waited three days to leave or chase after him, or whatever I was doing?

Every time I answered one question, I seemed to come up with ten more. Instead of alleviating my frustration, I was multiplying it.

My passport was tucked into the back cover of the day planner. I pulled it out and flipped it open.

The passport photo was marginally better than the one on

my driver's license. The passport itself had been through the wringer. It was stamped by customs officials in at least seven countries. I had taken four trips to Mexico, three to Canada, two to England, and one each to Jamaica, Spain, Kenya, and the Bahamas. Based on the dates on the stamps, my most recent trips out of the country had been the year before to Kenya and the jaunt to Jamaica the year before that. That trip had probably been for my honeymoon.

The most important two weeks of my life and I couldn't remember a single detail about them.

I returned the passport to its hiding place, zipped up the day planner, and shoved it back into the pack. Three items remained in the main compartment: a portable DVD player, a DVD of *The Usual Suspects*, and a dog-eared copy of the collected short stories of Ernest Hemingway.

I flipped the DVD box over to read the description of the movie. The plot sounded serpentine, one I wouldn't be able to follow with one eye on the screen and the other in the backpack. I decided to save the movie for later—when I could watch it on a larger screen and with a clearer head. I put it away, along with the portable player.

I turned to the book. A business card was stuck between the end of "In Another Country" and the beginning of "Hills Like White Elephants." I seized the card, thinking (hoping?) it might offer me another clue to my identity.

"Larry's Lube" the card read. "Keeping You Wet Since 1936."

Not much help there.

I replaced the makeshift bookmark and flipped through the pages. I—or someone else—had highlighted vast sections of the collection and made copious notes in the margins as if the stories were something to be analyzed and deconstructed and not merely enjoyed.

"A writer should be a person on whom nothing is lost."

The voice was my own; the words felt like someone else's. Like something that had been drummed into me in high school English class.

Like the day planner, the back cover of the book contained its own hidden treasure. A piece of cream-colored stationery was folded in half and tucked behind the last page. I unfolded the note. The paper was plain, devoid of logos or personalization—depriving me of any obvious clues to its origin.

The body of the note was brief, written in a scrawling, hurried script that was barely legible. A doctor's handwriting. Cryptic but shattering, the note said simply, "I won't be the lie you tell." It was signed not with a name but an initial—J.

J for Jack.

I didn't have any samples of his handwriting, but I didn't need physical proof to support what my heart knew to be true: Jack had written the note. The evidence leading me to that conclusion was overwhelming. The single ticket. His absence. The tentative "anniversary in June?" The desperate "talk to him!!"

We were having problems and the stress had…The stress had…

Turning my face toward the window, I fought to regain control. If I cried now, I might not stop.

I told myself not to jump to conclusions. There were a hundred possible explanations for the note—and probably as many suspects. The correct one might not be the most obvious.

Cloud cover obstructed my view of the ground. Somewhere below me, people were living their lives while I was trying to pick up the shattered pieces of mine.

"Take your own advice," I told myself. "*Talk* to him."

CHAPTER TWO

I stood in front of the luggage carousel watching the baggage go around in circles. According to the claim ticket affixed to the back of my boarding pass, I had checked two pieces of luggage. Without examining every bag, how would I know which two were mine? I would have to wait it out. If I let the other passengers go first, whatever they left behind would most likely be mine.

I stepped away from the carousel, allowing the people who knew what they were looking for to grab their bags and head outside to find ground transportation. I moved to a bench a few feet away and waited for the crowd to thin out.

I tried to figure out how the high-tech cell phone worked. Fortunately, the Power and Menu buttons were clearly marked. Otherwise, I might have spent all afternoon watching music videos on an endless loop.

I called the number listed for the vacation house but got the answering machine. "Hello," a computer-generated voice intoned, "we're unable to take your call right now. Please leave a message and—"

I ended the call and dialed the next number on my list. The one saved in the phone's directory as "Home." No answer there, either.

I scrolled down to "Jack Work," but the phone rang before I could dial the number. The display panel read "Jack Cell." *He* was calling *me*.

I put the phone to my ear. "Hello?" I asked tentatively, only to have the phone ring again. The ringer was set to a samba beat, which could have been fun in other circumstances, but was profoundly annoying in my present one.

I pressed buttons at random, hoping one would let the incoming call through without cutting it off.

"Hello?" I said again.

Jack's voice was deep and soothing—as if he should be churning out audiotapes to help insomniacs fall asleep instead of practicing medicine. "So you *have* landed. You said you were going to call me the minute you touched down."

His palpable relief at hearing from me threw me even further off balance. He didn't sound like the author of a Dear Jane letter speaking to its recipient.

If he hadn't written the note, who had?

"I—I was about to call you," I stammered, "but you beat me to it."

"It's about time I beat you at something. Do you have any idea how emasculating it is for me to have my wife be a better athlete than I am?" he asked with a chuckle. "At least I'm better with my hands. I do have that going for me. How's the weather down there?" He answered before I could. "To die for, I bet." He sighed. "I wish you had let me come with you."

So traveling alone had been *my* idea. But why? If things were normal between us, wouldn't I have wanted him with me?

"Are we happy?" I asked.

He didn't answer right away. When he did respond, his jovial, self-effacing tone was nowhere to be found. He sounded concerned. More than that, he sounded scared.

"You are my best friend, my lover, and my wife. I have loved you from the moment I saw you. I love you more than anything else in the world," he said. "When you told me you wanted to spend some time on your own, you said you needed to get your head together but it had nothing to do with us. Has something happened to change that?"

"I wish I knew."

"What does that mean?"

"It means I don't know who I am," I said. "I don't know what's going on with me and I need time to figure it out."

"I knew this would happen. It was noble of you to quit the firm the way you did—you'll always be a hero to a lot of people for taking a stand when no one else would—but how are you going to replace the thrill you get when you're trying a case no one except you thinks you can win?"

Speaking in a rush as if he were afraid he might forget something if I interrupted him, he didn't give me time to answer his question.

"You agreed to chair the fund-raising committee this year, and I'm sure you'll twist as many arms as it takes to reach the administration's stated goal, but, my little adrenaline junkie, hospital politics won't provide adequate excitement for you. You're too independent to be a housewife so don't even think about giving that a try. Before you say it, I know staying at home all day was good enough for our mothers, but you aren't your mother—or mine, thank God. Our legal department might be contacting you to see if you'd like to join our team of in-house counsels, but don't feel obligated to say yes if you don't want to. You *are* allowed to have a life that's separate from mine."

"I just want a life," I said. "At the moment, any will do."

Either he couldn't hear or he chose to ignore the desperation in my voice.

"A cynic would say you're too young to be having a mid-life crisis," he said. "Speaking as a cockeyed optimist—one that's hopelessly in love with you, I might add—I'm telling you to take all the time you need. But when you find the answers you're looking for, make sure they lead you back here." He paused, then surged forward. "All I want is to make you happy, Sydney. I told you that when we were dating. I told you that when I asked you to marry me, and I'm telling you again now. Forget what my mother said. We don't have to have a baby right now. She's waited this long to be a grandmother. What difference would a few more years make?"

I hadn't thought of children until he mentioned them. I was grateful to hear that we didn't have any. I didn't think I could bear the thought of not knowing anything about them. Of not remembering the day they were born. The day they spoke their first words. The day they took their first steps. It would have been too much.

"If you want to go back to work, that's fine with me," Jack continued. "Whatever you decide to do, I will support you one hundred percent. You know that, don't you?"

Even though I'd essentially just met him, he had me convinced. He was a man with my best interests at heart. And he loved me so much I could feel it through the phone.

"Yes, I know." His support seemed to be limitless and unconditional. I thought I could trust him, but nagging doubts prevented me from letting him in on my secret. "I feel so lost, Jack," I said, my resolve weakening. "Help me."

"I wish you would let me help you with this." He sounded as frustrated as I did. "But I know you're only asking now to humor me. Your stubborn streak is the stuff of legend. Just know that I'm here for you."

"I do."

"And don't think too hard. Sometimes we can go around our elbows to get to the truth when the truth is staring us right in the face. We just have to open our eyes and see it. Or find the courage to admit that we've known it all along. I hope you find your truth. And that it still involves me. I love you, Syd."

"I love you, too" didn't feel right and "Thank you" didn't feel appropriate so I said nothing.

The amount of information he had given me was dizzying. I would have to sort through a dozen possible reasons in order to find the one that had sent me over the edge.

After I ended the call, I scrolled through the directory again. I highlighted the entry saved as "Jen Home." It was time to put that best friends for life theory to the test.

The phone was picked up on the second ring.

"This is Marcus," the voice on the other end said.

Not expecting anyone else to answer, I nearly hung up. "Is Jen there?" I asked cautiously.

"Oh, hi, Syd," Marcus replied, recognizing my voice. "No, she's off saving the world again."

"I thought she just got home." According to the notation in the day planner, I'd thrown a party to mark that occasion just four days before.

"She did. She was supposed to be home for a month, but she decided not to stay that long. As she put it, she wanted to be someplace she could do some good. Everyone needs a purpose in life. I think it's safe to say that Jen has found hers. I suppose I should be grateful—her organization does wonderful things over there—but all I do is worry about her, not the people she's trying to save. I have a hard time believing she didn't tell you she was leaving. You two tell each other everything."

He sounded skeptical. As if I were testing him and he didn't know why.

"She might have mentioned it to me," I said, trying to cover, "but I have so much going on right now that I don't know which end is up."

"I hear you. She probably thought you would have tried to talk her out of it, anyway."

"I'd love to talk to her."

"To beg her to come to her senses and come home to a nice, cushy private practice? I've already tried that. It didn't work."

"Even so, is there a number where I can reach her?" In the address book, her cell phone number had been crossed out. Had she changed it and not given me her new one? That didn't sound like something a best friend would do.

"In the middle of the desert?" he scoffed. "I don't think so. E-mail's your best bet. Considering she doesn't check it every day, even that takes a while. If she gets her hands on a sat phone, though, and deigns to check in with me, I'll tell her to give you a call. But you two are as thick as thieves. You always have been. It still amazes me that Jack was able to pry you apart long enough for your father to walk you down the aisle. If you think she's going to call me before she calls you, you're dreaming."

"But she might not know where to reach me."

"The vacation house, right?"

I started. How much had I told him? How well did I know him? If he were my best friend's husband, very. He would have had to meet with my approval—just as Jack would have had to meet with Jennifer's.

"Are you okay, Syd?" Marcus asked. "You don't sound like yourself."

That was the understatement of the year.

"I'm fine," I lied. "I just wish I'd had more time with her, that's all."

"You and me both. I assume you heard about the verdict. Ten years, huh?"

Ten years? What was he talking about? Then I remembered the headline I had seen during the flight from Chicago. Something about the Subway Slasher. Had I been involved with the case in some way? How was that possible when Jack said I had quit the firm I worked for?

"Looks like the powers-that-be should have listened to you. When they call begging you to come back to the fold—and you know they will—I hope you hold out for a six-figure raise. You deserve it after what they put you through. I'd better go. I have to plug a hole in a client's firewall before a hacker tries to walk through it. Take care, Syd."

He hung up and I wandered back over to the luggage carousel. The number of bags to choose from had dwindled to a more manageable sum. I found mine with little effort. As I headed outside to hail a cab, I reflected on my conversation with Marcus—and what it meant.

J for Jennifer?

It was theoretically possible, but it made no sense. Not if we were as close as Marcus said we were. Then again, I had no way of knowing if she'd told me about her sudden departure or if she'd kept me in the dark. If we'd had a rift, she could have written the note.

Cars, taxis, and shuttle buses fought for space in the tiny parking lot. From the outside, the squat one-story airport looked more like a strip mall—minus the hair salons and nail shops. I headed for the cab at the head of the line. The driver leaned against his car, a bright yellow Chevrolet Caprice with advertisements for traveling road shows painted on both of its rear doors. Dressed in sandals, a garish Hawaiian shirt, and knee-length shorts, the cabbie looked readier for vacation than I did.

As he stowed my luggage in the generous trunk, I slid into the roomy backseat. I pulled forty dollars out of my wallet to pay for the cab ride so I wouldn't have to flash my money in front of him later.

He climbed into the front seat and slammed the door. "Where are you headed?" he asked, turning on the meter as he pulled away from the curb.

I gave him the address of the house on United Street.

"Sure thing." He flipped through several radio stations before settling on one that was playing upbeat reggae. "Is this all right?"

"It's fine."

I pulled out the note and took another look at it. The message was unchanged.

I won't be the lie you tell.

Jack said I was searching for the truth. I thought I might be better served trying to uncover a lie.

Chapter Three

The cab driver dropped me off in front of the house on United Street but didn't see me in. He deposited my bags on the porch and left to pick up another fare. It was just as well. I didn't want him to see me fumbling with the keys as I tried to find the one that fit the front door. He might have had a few questions for me. Questions I wouldn't be able to answer.

The front door sported two locks, the ring in my hand four keys. I tried each key in succession until I found the right combination that fit the locks. The tedious process tested what little patience I had left.

A four-digit number was taped to the back of the key that turned the deadbolt. I quickly found out why. The security alarm screeched to life when I opened the door. The alarm code had probably been ingrained in my memory less than twelve hours before. It, like everything else, was lost in the fog that had enveloped my brain.

Unprepared for a confrontation with the police, I tried to stem the tide of rising panic within me. I turned to the keys clutched tightly in my fist. I punched the handwritten numbers into the control panel next to the front door and prayed they were the right ones.

My prayers were answered. The alarm immediately fell silent.

I pulled my bags inside the house, then closed and locked the door. I stripped off my shirts—both of them—and dropped them on the floor. Then I kicked off my boots. My wool socks were plastered to my skin. I peeled those off, too. As I walked around, I could trace each step I made via the prints my sweaty feet left on the dark wood floor.

The temperature controls were in a hallway off from the small kitchen. The thermostat was set to an energy-conserving eighty degrees. I cranked it down to a more comfortable seventy-two.

With one mission accomplished, I put my hands on my hips and wondered what to do next.

"I'm here," I said to the empty living room. "Now what?"

I took a quick tour of the house to acclimate myself to my surroundings.

The living room was spacious and open, filled with bright floral-print furniture. The massive entertainment center was the focal point of the room. Flanked by built-in bookcases that displayed books on one side and movies on the other, it housed a wide-screen TV, a CD player, and a home theater system. Strategically placed speakers throughout the room gave the term "surround sound" new meaning.

The kitchen contained the bare essentials—sink, refrigerator, stove, dishwasher. The exterior of the refrigerator was decorated with magnets collected from the string of islands that made up the Florida Keys—Elliott Key, Key Largo, Tavernier, Islamorada, Indian Key, Long Key, Marathon, Bahia Honda, Big Pine Key, and, finally, Key West. Each magnet was accompanied by photos that documented the purchase. There were at least a dozen pictures of me or Jack and sometimes both of us, grinning from ear to ear as we exited a convenience store, gas station, or gift shop with another find in our hands.

Even though the face in half the pictures was mine—and I'd been behind the camera for the other half—I felt like I was eavesdropping on someone else's life. Like I was invading my own privacy. I'd had the same feeling on the plane when I'd read the day planner. I tried to convince myself that it was a necessary evil. A part of the process I'd have to undergo in order to reclaim who I was.

Unlike the crowded front, the interior of the refrigerator was empty, which meant I would have to find a grocery store sooner or later. I opted for later.

I headed down the hall again. A door on the left led to the guest bedroom, which was decorated in a mélange of tropical colors that were as loud as my cab driver's shirt had been. The walls were the color of orange sherbet, the bedding was lime green, and the throw rugs were aquamarine. I didn't know whether to cover my eyes or my ears.

The bathroom, in contrast, was muted, with a pervasive nautical theme that encompassed everything from the rugs to the shower curtain to the toothbrush holder to the sand dollar–covered wallpaper.

The half-bathroom on the other side of the hall seemed like something of an afterthought. Unlike the other rooms, which contained several breathtaking photographs of the beach, its beige walls were unadorned.

The master bedroom was at the end of the hall. The white four-poster bed stood out in sharp contrast to the ocean blue walls. French doors led to the patio and backyard. A pool covered by a blue tarp beckoned me.

"First things first."

I retrieved my suitcases from the living room and dragged them down the hall.

I unzipped the sturdy Samsonite bags and began to unpack while I sat cross-legged on the floor. I sorted through the neatly folded clothes. Pile after pile of T-shirts, tank tops, shorts, jeans, bathing suits, and swimsuit cover-ups joined me on the floor. I felt like the recipient of an unexpected shopping spree. Until I reminded myself that all the "new" things that surrounded me were my own. Things I had bought and paid for months, if not years, before.

The garish guest bedroom aside, at least I had good taste.

After I put the clothes away—I stowed some in the closet and some in the white cottage-style dresser at the foot of the bed—I opened the French doors and walked outside. I made a beeline for the small pool. I knelt next to it, lifted the cover, and stuck one hand in the water to test the temperature. It was colder than I'd expected but not cold enough to keep me out.

Trying not to spill any of the leaves that had settled on it since it was put into place, I pulled the cover off the pool and laid it aside. The tall fence surrounding the backyard afforded me complete privacy, so I discarded the rest of my clothes and dove naked into the frigid water.

"Last one in's a rotten egg!"

The voice in my head was my brother's. The shock of recognition turned my swan dive into a belly flop. I surfaced gasping for air, the chlorinated water burning my nasal passages. I held on to the side of the pool as I tried to clear my lungs.

My first swimming lesson. Patrick was eight; I was six. He had taken to swimming right away and already had a year of lessons under his belt. We were at one of the public pools in Wheaton, our hometown. I remembered my fear of the water and Patrick's noble attempts to put me at ease. I remembered the instructor, an eager young man whose main goal in life was to drop out of college and move to California to become a lifeguard. I remembered my parents watching from the sidelines, the expressions on their faces a mixture of anxiety and pride.

I remembered.

Not everything. Just bits and pieces from my childhood. My first pets—a pair of goldfish named Bert and Ernie that had both gone belly up after six months. My first real Christmas—Santa brought me an EASY-BAKE Oven and I spent the afternoon churning out miniature cakes that Patrick scarfed down as soon as I could frost them. Patrick ended up with a stomachache and I ended up with an aversion to baking. Now when I want to satisfy my sweet tooth, I leave the preparation to the experts.

Like the flashes in the airport, these memories had come when I stopped obsessing over my situation and allowed myself to think of something else. Trying to prompt more recollections, I kept swimming until my arms felt like they were going to fall off my shoulders, but none came.

I dragged myself out of the pool exhausted but hopeful.

"I'm not a lost cause yet," I told myself as I gathered my clothes. "I *can* do this on my own."

Famous last words?

Chapter Four

I took a shower to wash the chlorine out of my hair. After I dried off, I pulled on a white terrycloth robe I found hanging in the closet. I wanted to take a look at the cache of home videos that lined the bookcase to the right of the entertainment center, but hunger got the best of me.

I put on a pink Oxford shirt and a pair of navy blue Duck Head shorts. I traded in my heavy boots for airy brown sandals. I activated the alarm that had given me such pause earlier, locked the front door, and headed down the steps. I took a left when I reached the sidewalk. According to the guidebook that rested on the coffee table in the living room, United Street crossed Duval, the crowded stretch of road that was Key West's main drag for tourists. Bars, restaurants, and art galleries lined both sides of the thoroughfare.

A few blocks from the house, down on South Street, was the Atlantic Shores, an oceanfront resort for gay men. A couple of blocks past that, back on United, was Pearl's Rainbow, a sprawling guesthouse for women. I could hear the sound of music and raucous laughter drifting over the high privacy fence that surrounded the property. Good fences might make good neighbors, but they also make curious ones. I'm sure I wasn't alone in wondering what went on on the other side of this one.

On the street, rainbow flags flew everywhere. I wondered whose idea it had been to purchase a house so close to a gay enclave—mine, Jack's, or our real estate agent's.

As I approached the former home of The Chicken Store on the corner of United and Duval, a woman on a Day-Glo yellow scooter slowed to check me out. Since scooters were the primary mode of transportation on the island, I couldn't tell if she were a tourist or a local.

She wore an orange bikini top and a pair of skimpy denim cutoffs. The bulging muscles in her firm bronze thighs were thick and corded, as if she worked them out constantly. Her feet were shod, if you could call it that, in thick-soled flip-flops. A pair of interlocked women's symbols was tattooed on the outside of her right ankle. Her evenly tanned skin displayed no tan lines. Either she worked in the sun or spent a great deal of time playing underneath it.

"Need a ride?" she asked.

"No, I'm fine, thanks."

I kept walking. She shadowed me. "A tour guide then?"

"I think I can handle it by myself."

I made a right turn. She followed suit. Combing her brown hair with her fingers, she pulled her wraparound sunglasses off her face and perched them on top of her head. Her blue eyes sparkled in my direction. "Are you sure?"

I held up my left hand so she could see my wedding ring. "I'm married."

"Married doesn't mean dead," she replied.

"But it does mean committed."

"I always thought commitment was for asylums. I'm Marcy. If you change your mind about that whole commitment thing, I'll be around."

"I'll keep that in mind."

She smiled, revealing peach pit dimples in both cheeks. "See you at the sunset celebration?"

Every night in Mallory Square, tourists and locals joined the area's artists, street performers, and musicians to celebrate the end of another day in paradise. "Maybe," I said noncommittally. I was flattered by the attention but not interested. The last thing I needed was a vacation fling.

She smiled again. "See you there." She revved the scooter's engine and did a U-turn, speeding off in the other direction. Mallory Square was at the beginning of Duval; she was headed for the end.

I didn't plan on taking her up on her offer to help me forgo my commitment to Jack. Even though I couldn't remember it, I had made it. Nevertheless, her proposal intrigued me. Trying not to draw attention, I'd kept my head down all day. I'd barely given myself a second glance, let alone anyone else. But, on some level, I was attracted to her. Whether it was her carefree attitude or her killer thighs, I wanted to see her again.

The fact that I was married made it easy for me to assume that I was heterosexual, but it didn't guarantee it. I wondered if Marcy had stopped to talk to me because she saw me as a kindred spirit or as just another pretty face.

I wondered, too, how I saw myself. Was I gay? Was I straight? Was I bi? Something as fundamental as my sexuality didn't seem like something I could forget. Yet I was as much in the dark about it as I was about everything else.

Chapter Five

Being surrounded by water put me in the mood for seafood. I headed to Jimmy Buffett's Margaritaville for some blackened mahi-mahi. While I ate, I was entertained by diners performing their off-key renditions of Jimmy's greatest hits. After dinner, I walked the length of Duval Street to burn off the calories. I did a little bit of window shopping but not much. I didn't want souvenirs. I wanted memories. My memories.

I felt drawn to Sloppy Joe's but resisted the urge to go in. When he lived on the island, Ernest Hemingway had made the bar his favorite hangout. The six-hundred-plus page book in my backpack told me I was a Hemingway fan. If that were true, logic dictated that the legendary establishment was one of my favorite hangouts, too. Which meant, more than likely, that they knew me there. I couldn't take that chance. Not until I was myself again. Sipping a rum and Coke in the Hog's Breath Saloon, I wondered what I'd do if that didn't happen. Would I return to my old life or try to forge a new one?

Yet another thing for me to figure out. Good thing I wasn't on a timetable.

The sun set while I was sitting in the Hog's Breath, but I headed to Mallory Square anyway. I wasn't expecting—or hoping—to run into Marcy. At least, I didn't think I was. I simply wanted to get a feel for the place. To see if all the eccentric behavior I'd read about was real or an urban legend created to sell visitors' guides and lure gullible tourists.

Walking into the square, I was greeted by the sight of a homeless man sleeping on a wooden bench. His right hand held a firm grip on the handlebars of a battered blue bicycle. The bike's kickstand was up, which meant the bike could crash to the ground if its owner rolled over or let go. A white bulldog wearing heart-shaped sunglasses sat panting happily in a basket attached to the bike's rear wheel.

So much for urban legends.

I joined a crowd that had gathered to watch a man and a woman covered in gray body paint juggle daggers with eight-inch blades. The knives' sharp metal edges glistened in the lamplight. To enhance the sense of danger even more, the painted pair tossing the weapons back and forth were shirtless. The silver rings that pierced their nipples pealed like tiny bells each time their taut arms moved.

A few feet away from the topless twosome, I listened to a one-man band play songs from Madonna's catalog. His rendition of "Like A Virgin" was one I'll definitely never forget.

Considering my present circumstances, perhaps I should rephrase that.

I moved over by the water so I could watch the waves roll in.

"Looking for me?"

Marcy's voice in my ear made me jump. I took a step back. She felt too close. "No, I wasn't."

"Are you sure?" She was wearing the same shorts I'd seen her in earlier, but her bikini top and flip-flops were gone, replaced by a form-fitting cycling jersey and a pair of Nikes.

"You don't give up, do you?"

She smiled. "Not when I see something I want."

"Something you want or something you can't have?"

Her smile grew. "We'll see about that," she said. "Having fun?" She indicated the wide variety of performers that dotted the square and their captive audiences.

"Yeah, it's pretty cool down here, but I'm about ready to call it a night. It's been a long day for me."

"Ready for that ride yet?" she asked. "My pedi-cab's right over there."

She pointed behind her to a three-wheeled vehicle that was parked near the entrance to the square. So that explained both her tan and her great legs.

"How much is the fare?"

"That's negotiable. Why don't we figure it out when we get there?" I didn't bite. "Okay," she said, holding up her hands. "It's twenty-five dollars an hour, the base rate's fifteen. Unless, of course, you tell me you're staying on one of the other islands. Then we really would have to do some negotiating."

I eased her mind. "No, I'm staying close to where you saw me this afternoon."

"Then shall we?"

I followed her to the pedi-cab and climbed in the backseat. She stood on the pedals to create enough force to get the wheels moving. She sat down once we were under way.

I guess I should have passed on dessert. On second thought, the key lime pie I'd had was worth the extra pound or two.

"Are you staying at Pearl's?" Marcy asked, half-turning in her seat.

"Not quite."

"Oh, that's right. You're married. Too many lesbians hang out there." She took one hand off the handlebars and shook her left arm. The rubber rainbow bracelet on her wrist slid toward her elbow but quickly resumed its former position when she reached for the bottle of water clamped to the bar between her legs. She offered me a sip, but I shook my head.

"You enjoy teasing me, don't you?"

She grinned, flashing those peach pit dimples again. "I would enjoy doing a lot of things to you if you'd let me." She returned the water to its holder.

I turned my attention to a bearded man wearing black motorcycle boots, tight jeans, black leather chaps, and white angel wings. "I think that's my cue."

"To do what?" Marcy asked.

I turned back to her so she wouldn't think I was avoiding the issue at hand. "To end this conversation."

"Why? Am I getting too close? Am I making you uncomfortable?"

"You're coming on a bit strong." I held on to the sides of the carriage as she braked for a red light.

"That's not an answer," she shot back. "Neither is 'I'm married.'"

She was challenging me. I wasn't sure if I liked it. "What do you consider an answer?"

Her eyes bored into me. "That depends on the question, now, doesn't it?"

"What's your question?" I asked, afraid of what her answer would be.

"I have several, but I'll start with an easy one." The light turned green again. "What's your name?" she asked once we were under way again.

I told her.

"And where's your husband tonight, Sydney?"

I told her that, too.

So much for the easy ones. I hoped the degree of difficulty on the hard ones would be relatively low. I didn't want to lie to her or be forced to make something up. Which, I suppose, were one and the same.

"And what does he do in Chicago?"

"He's a doctor," I said, hoping she wouldn't ask me what kind. I didn't know. He could have been anything. I felt increasingly uncomfortable. The ride wasn't that far, but it seemed like it would never end. Sharing the narrow road with cars, scooters, and bicycles was nerve-wracking, too. I kept expecting one of them to turn us into road kill. I felt exposed—in more ways than one.

"What about you?" Marcy pressed.

"I'm a doctor's wife."

"Besides that."

"I'm still working on that one."

She looked at me over her shoulder as she turned left on United Street. "Now *that* is an answer."

The traffic on United wasn't as heavy as that on Duval. With fewer obstacles to dodge, Marcy covered the ten blocks in about ten seconds. She left the pedi-cab at the curb while she walked me to my door.

"What are you doing tomorrow?" she asked.

"Grocery shopping. My cupboards are bare."

"What about after that?"

I unlocked the deadbolt and stepped inside to shut off the alarm. "I haven't planned that far ahead yet." Standing in the half-open doorway, I held one hand on the knob. I was hoping she'd get the hint without making me appear rude by asking her to leave.

"Would you like to have dinner?" she asked. "Maybe go dancing? Or better yet, we could get up early, catch a cat, and go snorkeling. The water's crystal clear and the coral's beautiful."

Confused by her terminology, I assumed cat meant

catamaran, not Morris or Garfield or one of their six-toed stray cousins I'd seen running around. "I shouldn't."

"Why?" She shoved her hands in the back pockets of her cutoffs. "Do you have something against snorkeling?"

"No, but I don't want to lead you on." She seemed so excited about the prospect of being with me that I had to put a stop to it.

"I think I'm the one who's doing the leading here, don't you?" She didn't wait for me to answer the question. "I know you're married, Sydney. Even though I'm attracted to you, I can respect that. The fact that you're straight and married and I'm gay and unattached doesn't stop us from being friends, does it?"

Finally, another easy question. "No, it doesn't. It might even make it easier."

She grinned as if I'd said something amusing, profound, or incredibly naïve. "Then I'll see you in the morning?"

Her enthusiasm broke down my defenses. "What time?"

Her face brightened. "I'll pick you up here at seven thirty."

I grimaced. "That early?"

"If you want to beat the crowd, it's a necessary evil, I'm afraid. We have to drive to the Seaport to charter a catamaran— if they're not all taken—then follow that up with a forty-minute boat ride to the reef. But once we get there, we can take as long as we want."

"Then seven thirty it is." I tightened my grip on the doorknob. "I'd better get to bed and you'd better get back to work."

"I have a confession to make." She leaned toward me and motioned for me to follow suit. When I did, she said in a conspiratorial whisper, "Today's my day off."

"So the cab ride was—"

"An opportunity to spend some time with you." She smiled sheepishly. "Are we still on for tomorrow?"

"Only if you promise to be honest with me from now on. If we're to be friends, I'd like to believe that I can trust you."

"You can."

"Prove it to me."

"How?"

"Answer a question for me."

"Anything. What do you want to know?"

"What do you want from me?"

She didn't hesitate. "Everything you have to give."

CHAPTER SIX

When Marcy left, I didn't go to bed like I'd said I would. I went to work. She might have had the night off, but I didn't.

A thick medical encyclopedia lay on the banquette in the kitchen. I used it to perform a quick bit of self-diagnosis.

There were seven types of amnesia to choose from.

Anteretrograde amnesia was marked by the inability to remember ongoing events after the incidence of trauma or the onset of the disease that caused the condition.

Because I remembered everything that had happened since I found myself running through O'Hare, I ruled that out.

Korsakoff's syndrome was memory loss caused by chronic alcoholism.

I wasn't craving a bottle of vodka or shaking uncontrollably from the DT's so I ruled that one out, too.

Lacunar amnesia was the inability to remember a specific event.

Close, but no cigar—unless my entire life counted as a specific event.

Posthypnotic amnesia seemed like a bit of a stretch. Unless someone had drugged me, I didn't see myself being able to relax enough to fall for the dangling watch on a chain and the old "You are getting very sleepy." I was too much of a type-A personality for that.

That left three possibilities.

Transient global amnesia, spontaneous memory loss that could last from minutes to several hours, seemed like the likeliest suspect—until I read the part about it being usually seen in middle-aged to elderly people. I didn't fit in either of those categories. Not yet, anyway.

Retrograde amnesia was the inability to remember events that occurred prior to the onset of amnesia.

"Sufferers do not lose all their memories," I read. "Usually, the memory loss is worst for events just before the injury. Events from long ago are more likely to be safe."

That could explain why I remembered being eight but not eighteen.

Based on what I read, if I had amnesia of the retrograde variety, I wouldn't ever remember what had caused my memory loss or the events leading up to it. Caused by brain injury or disease, retrograde amnesia didn't seem likely, though. My head was still attached to my shoulders and I felt fine physically. A little full from dinner, but otherwise fine.

That left emotional/hysterical amnesia, memory loss caused by psychological trauma. I latched on to that one. It seemed to fit and, more importantly, it was described as being "usually temporary." I liked that part best of all.

I dressed for bed but went into the living room. The home movies in the bookcase were sorted by date. I didn't pull out the earliest one. Those memories were coming back on their own. Instead, I skipped to the ones that covered the periods that were still missing from my mind: high school and beyond.

I took a tape titled "Senior Prom, April 1996" off the shelf and slid it into the VCR side of the DVD/VCR combo while I tuned the TV to channel three. I grabbed the VCR remote off the coffee table and sat on the couch. A sticky linoleum floor and a tub of hot buttered popcorn would have made for the perfect movie-going experience. I had neither. What I had was a date with my newfound friend: the unknown.

Shaky images filled the TV screen.

Patrick had manned the camera. As he sneaked up the stairs of our parents' house, he provided whispered narration like a nature photographer trying not to spook his subject.

At the top of the stairs, he turned the camera on himself. The low angle made him look ten feet tall. Since he was only five feet nine, he would have liked that. He had made the video when he was a nineteen-year-old sophomore at the University of Illinois. I'd followed him there a year later. He had majored in sports medicine; I had chosen pre-law. Currently, he was a member of the Chicago Bears' medical staff. I was a mystery wrapped inside an enigma—or however the saying goes.

How did I know all that? The images on the screen brought it back to me.

My life was finally coming into focus. Eager for more of the same, I moved closer to the TV set like a kid watching Saturday morning cartoons over a bowl of sugar-laden cereal.

"We're here to observe the mating—sorry, Mom and Dad—I mean *dating* habits of one Sydney Paulsen," Patrick said into the camera, sounding like the late Steve Irwin doing his typically manic voiceover on an old episode of *Crocodile Hunter*. "Today we will be witnessing a ritual known as prom night. Observe."

Turning the camera around again, Patrick continued down the hall. He stopped in front of a door that looked vaguely familiar. The Keep Out sign on the outside of the door had been amended to include the coda, "Patrick, this means YOU!!"

I remembered making the sign while Patrick and I were both in high school. When he went away to college, I hadn't bothered to take it down. It seemed he was around more when he didn't live at home than when he did.

Music and laughter seeped out of the closed door. Patrick opened the door, catching me and Jennifer *in flagrante delicto*—dancing deliriously in our pastel prom dresses to the dated strains of Los Del Rio. The duo's infectious song wouldn't sweep the U.S. until that summer, but I had gotten hooked on it during a family vacation to Mexico the year before.

I cringed at the sight of myself in big hair and yards of taffeta. I looked like a reject from a bad eighties music video. It was the nineties. Why hadn't I gotten the Rachel? If I had, the images of the old me dancing the Macarena wouldn't have been nearly as damaging to my psyche—or was that my ego?

Jennifer and I were halfway through our performance before we realized Patrick was in the room.

Hearing his devious laughter, Jen wheeled and fired her hairbrush at his head. He ducked, but not fast enough. The brush caught him squarely between the eyes and he went down, yelping in pain. The camera clattered to the floor but kept recording, capturing the sight of Patrick rolling around on the floor as if the bruise on his forehead was life threatening.

"What's going on up there?" my father called from downstairs.

"Nothing, Dad!" I shouted back.

"Stop whining, Pat," Jennifer chided, dragging him into the room by his feet. The back of his head banged on the threshold and he howled anew. I stepped over him and closed the door. Jennifer bent and picked up the camera. Her face filled the frame. "Show's over."

The screen went black. When the video picked up again, the venue had changed from my bedroom to the living room. The camera panned from my mother performing a quick patch job on my hem to my father watching a Bulls game on TV to

Patrick sitting forlornly on the couch with one ice pack on the front of his head and another on the back.

"How's the boo-boo, Pat?" Jennifer asked from behind the camera.

He flipped her the bird, causing the ice pack on the back of his head to spill open and dribble ice down the back of his Madras shirt. The camera followed his hasty retreat to the bathroom.

Jennifer guffawed. "This just isn't your day, is it, Patty boy?"

He flipped her off again and slammed the door.

"Oh, you two," my mother said when Jennifer returned to the living room. "You know you have feelings for each other. Why don't you just admit it?"

"Yeah, Jen," the younger me said, stifling a giggle. "Why don't you?"

My smile intimated that Jennifer and I had discussed the subject in great detail. I couldn't remember the outcome of those conversations. Did she have a crush on my brother or he on her?

Whatever the outcome of those conversations had been, it didn't matter anyway. Patrick was married to the former Kristin Connelly from St. Louis. I liked her—even though she was a Cardinals fan—and I adored their two beautiful boys, my nephews Kris, nine, and Kevin, four.

It was funny. Funny strange, not funny ha ha. I was starting to remember everyone in my life except for the two that meant the most to me—my husband and my best friend. My memories of my family were crystal clear, but the ones of Jack and Jennifer were fuzzy at best.

On the tape, the doorbell rang, extricating Jennifer from an awkward situation and sending my mother into a tizzy. After glancing in the mirror to see how her hair looked, my mother rushed around the room straightening this and tidying that. She took the camera from Jennifer and handed it to my father. "Sid, take this." She knocked on the bathroom door. "Patrick, come out of there. It's time."

My father reluctantly gave up his basketball game. Just as reluctantly, my brother came out of the bathroom. My mother, acting as movie director, positioned me and Jennifer by the stairs and stopped to check on her hair again. I half-expected her to yell "Action!" before she opened the door.

Two teenage boys—one white, one black, both nervous—stood on the porch.

"David, Marcus," my mother said, greeting them effusively. "It's so good to see you. Come in! Come in!"

David was David DiNunzio, the captain of the swim team and the first boy I ever slept with. We dated for a year and a half. We broke up a couple of weeks before graduation. He wanted to be free when he got to college because, as he put it, "The poon there was growing on trees."

It looked like Jennifer and her high school sweetheart had remained an item—unless she had (has) a thing for guys named Marcus. The high school version had been quite a catch. Smart, funny, and male model–gorgeous, all the girls had lusted after him. In 1996, though, interracial dating wasn't as accepted as it would come to be. Most parents in my peer group had gently discouraged their kids from crossing the color line. None of them wanted to be the ones other families whispered about in church or gossiped about on the street.

Someone apparently forgot to tell Jennifer—and Marcus. Locking eyes, they smiled at each other as if they were the only two people in the room.

I watched the pinning of corsages and the mandatory photo session. There were a few shots of the game, too, as Dad, distracted by crowd noise coming from the TV, turned to see what the Bulls were up to. The video ended after David, Jennifer, Marcus, and I climbed into the back of our rented limo and rode away.

As I (vaguely) remembered it, the prom had been just okay. Nothing to write home about. After making the rounds and having our pictures taken for our parents' sake, if not our own, David and I had ditched it for the main event—the senior party in Bryan Woods. That had been something just short of a Roman orgy. The next day, empty beer bottles and filled condoms had littered the ground.

I didn't remember Jennifer and Marcus being there, but that didn't mean anything. They could have been there and I'd forgotten that, too. With no videotape evidence to prompt me, I couldn't be certain.

I rewound the tape, put it back in its box, and returned it to the shelf.

The next video was "Sydney's High School Graduation." Not in the mood for pomp and circumstance, I watched it on fast forward. I slowed only to watch my fellow graduates and me toss our mortarboards in the air and promise to remain best friends for life. (That sounded familiar.) Some of us had kept that promise. Most, including me, had not. I didn't know where half those people were—or who they had become. I had lost track of them years before I had lost track of myself.

There were many more tapes to choose from—videos chronicling every major moment in my life over the past twenty-five years. My college years were next. With my brain on overload, I didn't think I could handle another blast from the past. Besides, I already remembered college's high points—attending my first keg party, pledging a sorority—and a few of the low ones—tossing my cookies at that keg party and walking in on one of my sorority sisters blowing the guy that I'd told her I had a crush on.

If sleep were the poor man's medicine, perhaps all I needed was an eight-hour dose to cure my malady. My heart, filled with trepidation, wouldn't allow me to be that optimistic. Something told me that I'd be back in front of the TV screen in a few hours analyzing more stolen moments from my past.

I wanted to skip straight to my wedding video, but I was afraid to. Afraid not that I would derail the recovery process by proceeding out of chronological order, but afraid that I wouldn't be able to connect to those memories as easily as I had the others—and afraid that I would. After all, there had to be a reason why I was subconsciously blocking Jack and Jennifer out of my mind—and that reason couldn't be good.

Had they betrayed me by sleeping together? Or had I betrayed them?

I wasn't in a rush to find out.

Chapter Seven

The alarm clock woke me out of a sound sleep. Disoriented, I hit the snooze button and tried to get my bearings. Nothing looked right. Blue walls? The walls in my apartment were— Shit, what color *were* the walls in my apartment?

Pulling the covers up to my chin, I let out a whimper of fear.

The sound of roosters crowing in the distance brought me back. Key West was overrun by stray chickens. A volunteer group, The Rooster Rescue Team, had been formed to take in the birds that had been orphaned or injured. City officials had hired a chicken catcher to round up the rest, but he had quickly left his post when he realized the job was too big for one person to handle.

I was facing a similarly monumental task.

I had gone to sleep hoping everything would be fine when I woke up. It wasn't. I could remember the night before but not the week before. I could remember twenty years before but not two years before. Then again, that wasn't entirely true. I could remember some recent events in my life and most of the old ones.

What I couldn't remember was anything that had to do

with Jack or Jennifer, lending credence to my theory that whatever was wrong with me had to do with one—or both—of them. Since they took up so much of my life, that explained why so much of my life was missing.

I covered my face with my hands and took a deep breath, the no-frills version of breathing into a paper bag. The anxiety soon passed. Frustration took its place. I'd thought that I'd had a breakthrough the night before, only to wake up the next day to more of the same—and the fear that it would always be that way.

I pounded the bed with my fists.

"What did I do to deserve this? Why is this happening to me?" I cried, doing a fairly good impersonation of a petulant child.

It took me nearly twenty minutes to drag myself out of the pool of self-pity I was drowning in. When Marcy rang the doorbell, I was still in my robe and my eyes were puffy from crying.

Marcy's welcoming smile quickly deteriorated into a frown. She was probably wondering what she had gotten herself into. I couldn't blame her if she were also trying to figure a way to get herself out of it.

"Is this a bad time?" she asked.

"Yes, but come in anyway."

She came inside and closed the door behind her. "What's wrong?" she asked, touching my arm.

I pulled away from her. "If I get into it, I'll go off again."

My emotions were all over the place. Her obvious concern for me nearly reduced me to grateful tears.

She looked at me hard, examining my face. "It's probably none of my business," she said, "but are you and your husband having problems?"

Were we?

"We're—*I'm* taking a break right now," I replied as honestly as I could.

She hitched up her shorts—low-slung khaki Dickies with frayed hems. Her white baby doll tee stopped just shy of her navel. "Do you want to reschedule? We can do this another day if you want. I can give you a rain check if you need one."

"I don't need a rain check," I insisted. "I need *this*."

I needed *her*.

She probably would have been as shocked to hear it as I was to hear myself think it. But it was true. Even though I had just met her, she was the only certainty in my life. The only thing I could take at face value. The rest was smoke and mirrors, dependent upon the validity of the memories slowly trickling back into my faulty brain. The brief time I'd spent with Marcy had helped me forget about my problems. She had helped me to feel less alone during my self-imposed exile. Less like a freak who could barely remember her own name. On a day when I felt dead inside, her energy and good humor were two things I desperately needed.

"Give me five minutes," I said.

"Sure thing."

In the bedroom, I crammed sunscreen, a hat, and a couple of towels into my backpack, then tossed my robe on the bed and put on a black two-piece bathing suit. A T-shirt and a pair of shorts covered the swimsuit. I slid my feet slid into a pair of sports sandals. My reflection in the mirror over the dresser confirmed my suspicions: I looked awful. With no time to dab Preparation H on the bags under my eyes, I hid them behind a pair of Ray-Bans.

Marcy was sitting on the couch. When she saw me approach, she leaped to her feet. She was as anxious as I was.

I tried to ease the tension with a smile. "Ready to go?" I asked. I slid my arms through the backpack's straps.

"You bet."

Marcy's scooter was waiting by the curb. "What, no pedi-cab?" I teased her, trying to get back to where we'd left off the night before when my situation had felt less dire.

"Maybe later." She tried not to smile but failed. "The Seaport's only a couple of blocks from Duval. Do you want to walk or ride?"

"We're going to get enough exercise at the reef," I said. It was already hot and humid and it wasn't even eight o'clock yet. "Let's ride."

She fired up the engine. I slid in behind her. Unsure of the proper etiquette, I didn't know where to put my hands. Was I supposed to grip the seat, her shirt, or her? The basket behind me was also an option, but—depending on the length of the ride—I didn't feel like dislocating my shoulders just to maintain a sense of propriety.

"Hold on!" she said as we pulled away from the curb.

To keep from falling over backward, I gripped Marcy's sides with both hands. Just like the night before, she turned to check on me.

"Okay back there?"

I nodded. "Go faster," I said, sliding my hands to her waist. "I want to feel the wind in my face."

She gunned the accelerator and the scooter shot forward. Closing my eyes, I held on tight.

"It's down there," Marcy said, pointing to a sign advertising catamaran charters. She cupped her hands around her mouth. "Ahoy!"

At the pier, a woman with a tan even deeper and darker than Marcy's returned her greeting. She wore a Florida Marlins baseball cap pulled low over her eyes. Her shiny black hair fell past her shoulders, protecting the back of her neck from the brutal sun.

"That's Ana," Marcy said. "She'll be our captain today. *The Painted Lady* seats eight, but Ana said she'd take us out on our own. It'll be just the three of us. I kind of owe you after the trick I played on you last night, so this is on me, okay?"

I doubted the fifteen dollars she'd bilked me out of for the off-duty pedi-cab ride would even put a dent in the fee for the boat rental. If she and Ana were friends, though, perhaps they had worked something out.

"You won't get any arguments from me."

When we made it down to the dock, Marcy provided introductions.

At five foot three, Ana was all lean muscle and sinew. She wore a sleeveless shirt that showed off her burnished brown arms. A tattoo of the Puerto Rican flag waved proudly on her right bicep. She covered her dark green eyes with the mirrored sunglasses that rested on the bill of her cap. *"Hola,"* she said as we shook hands.

I'd barely said hello before Ana and Marcy began an extended conversation in Spanish. The only words I managed to catch were *magnifica* and *amigas*.

"What was all that about?" I asked while Ana prepared the cat for departure.

"She said she thinks you're cute, but I told her to keep her hands off because I met you first," Marcy replied. She made the short hop from the pier to the deck of the boat. She used hand signals to indicate to Ana that she was taking me below. "Then she asked if you and I were dating. I told her we were just friends."

I followed Marcy down the stairs. My vision blurred briefly as my eyes made the adjustment from the sun to the shade. We ended up in the master stateroom, a swanky affair tricked out with a built-in bar, a king-sized bed, and separate bathroom and shower compartments.

"Is she a friend of yours, too?" I dropped my backpack on the L-shaped leather couch.

"One of my best. We dated for six months, but that's over now."

I walked over to the sliding glass doors. Beyond them lay a gorgeous view of the harbor. "And you're still friends? I would think you'd be at each other's throats."

Marcy took off her T-shirt and shorts, revealing a pink string bikini. "Key West's a small island. You see the same people everywhere you go. When you break up with someone, you have only two options: be friends with them or move. I don't want to move."

I could sense her wanting to ask me something, but she held off. Instead, she took me on a tour of the living quarters. The master stateroom took up half of the space below deck; staterooms in the port and starboard hulls shared the other half. When the tour was over, I stripped to my bathing suit and followed Marcy upstairs. Ana was in the shaded captain's area, waiting behind the wheel.

"How's it coming?" Marcy asked.

"Ready whenever you are," Ana said.

Marcy turned to me. "Last chance to back out. Are you sure you want to do this?"

I guess it was my day to take the lead. "I'm sure," I said. "Let's go."

Chapter Eight

The Painted Lady sliced through the turquoise water at a brisk fifteen knots.

Marcy squeezed a line of sunscreen into the palm of her left hand and rubbed the protectant into the skin covering her rippled stomach. I was in shape, but I didn't look like *that*. Oh, to be twenty-five again.

Ana caught me admiring Marcy's body.

"You like what you see?" she asked with a wicked smile as she lowered the volume on the Shakira CD pumping out of the sound system.

"Easy, Ana," Marcy said, closing her eyes as the sun beat down on her already brown body.

"You, of all people, should know that I don't do anything easy, *cara*," Ana shot back.

The comment made Marcy blush. I couldn't tell if she was embarrassed for my sake or for her own. She and Ana had such an easy rapport that I wondered why they had broken up. Fortunately, I felt comfortable enough to ask, "Why aren't you still together?" I rolled onto my stomach to give my back a chance to bake.

Marcy shaded her face with an upraised hand. "Do you want to tell the story or do you want me to do it?"

"I can't talk and drive at the same time," Ana said, her eyes focused on the horizon, "so why don't you handle this one?"

"How long do we have?"

Ana checked the bulky diver's watch on her wrist. "Twenty minutes."

"So I guess I'll do the short version." Marcy reached into the cooler at our feet and pulled out a can of Red Bull. She drank half of it in one thirsty gulp. "We met at a potluck," she said, resting her elbows on her knees. She rolled the metal can back and forth between her palms. "I brought mac and cheese. Ana brought—" Memory failing, she turned to Ana for help. "What was it again?"

"*Arroz con pollo.* How could you forget? You had four helpings."

"Who's telling this story, me or you?" Marcy asked with a grin. "As I was saying before I was so rudely interrupted, Ana and I met at a potluck at a mutual friend's house about three years ago. I had just moved down from Tennessee. Ana had been here forever."

"Watch it," Ana said. "I know I'm older than you are, but not *that* much."

"Okay, maybe not forever," Marcy said, "but a long time, nevertheless. Is that better?" She turned to Ana for confirmation.

"*Mucho. Gracias.*"

"It was an instant attraction," Marcy continued. "We slept together way too soon. We fucked like rabbits for six months, then woke up one morning and realized we didn't want the same things in life. I was too young and—"

"I was too set in my ways," Ana said.

"But I've grown up since then," Marcy said.

"And I've learned to relax," Ana chipped in.

"So what's stopping you from giving it another go?" I asked.

Marcy shrugged. "Been there. Done that."

"Bought the T-shirt," Ana said.

Marcy finished the rest of the Red Bull and put the empty can in the cooler. "What about you?" she asked me. "How did you meet your husband?"

"Husband?" Ana asked, visibly surprised. "You mean you're—"

Marcy quieted her with a warning look, then turned back to me. "If it's not too painful for you to talk about, I mean."

I scrambled for a response. Should I tell her the truth—which was I didn't remember—or concoct a plausible lie—my ideal meet-cute? A lie would probably sound more credible, but I didn't want to blend fact and fiction. I was already having enough trouble staying on top of things.

"I'd rather not, if that's okay with you."

"It's fine," Marcy said. "But if you ever feel like you want to talk, I'm a good listener."

"Since when?" Ana asked.

"I always have been," Marcy said, defending herself. "You just never liked to share."

"I shared with you."

"Yeah, what position you liked or what you wanted for dinner."

Ana chuckled. "Well, what else is there?"

Ana cut the engine and pressed a switch that sent the battered steel anchor plunging into the water. I watched a thick chain play out of the side of the boat as it followed the attached anchor into the crystalline depths.

Ana reached for the key ring attached to her belt. Then she moved to the starboard side of the boat, where she kneeled and unlocked a panel that fit smoothly into the surface of the deck. She pulled out diving equipment—flippers, goggles, and fluorescent metal snorkels with black rubber tips on each end. Her movements were smooth and self-assured, despite the sometimes treacherous footing on the slippery deck.

"Are you coming in with us?" Marcy asked as Ana dropped the gear on top of the red and white Igloo.

Ana smiled down at her. "This is your date, not mine, *cara.*"

"It's not—"

Ana cut off Marcy's feeble protest with a wave of her hand. "I'll keep an eye on things up here. You two have fun." She gave us some basic pointers: breathe through your mouth and if you dive under, don't breathe at all.

Like I said. Real basic stuff.

Chapter Nine

I dangled my feet over the side of the boat and swung them back and forth a couple of times to gather the momentum I needed to propel myself forward. The water offered a shockingly cool contrast to the superheated air. As I dove under, colorful fish—tropical and otherwise—swam over to greet me. Marcy captured the moment with the underwater camera Ana had let us borrow. She gave me the thumbs up to let me know she had the shot.

We surfaced for air. I blew collected water out of my snorkel and went under again.

The reef was breathtaking. Dozens of tiny fish swam in and out of the coral's crevices. The colors were amazing. Brighter and more beautiful than those found in any paint store.

My body floated on the waves. I let my mind drift with it. All my cares, all my worries seemed far behind me. When Marcy floated past me squirting water out of her mouth like it was a whale's blowhole, I laughed so hard I almost drowned. How long had I been impersonating Atlas, walking around with the weight of the world on my shoulders?

When Ana announced it was time to go, I swam back to *The Painted Lady* as slowly as I could. I didn't want the trip to end.

A metal ladder attached to the side of the boat extended into the water. I got a good grip on the ladder with both hands before I attempted to climb up. Instead of making my way back to the deck, I felt as if I were ascending to the gallows.

For a few brief hours, I had been able to lock my problems away in a tightly sealed box and shut the lid. Now I would have to open that lid and deal with whatever flew out. The more I thought about it, the less certain I became that I wanted to find out what had happened to drive me so far from home. If I hadn't been able to deal with it the first time around, what made me think I would be able to the next time?

I envied Marcy's youthful exuberance. Her ability to make everything seem like a game. I wanted her to teach me how to play.

"Feel better?" Marcy asked as we removed our flippers.

"That was just what the doctor ordered," I replied. I planned to get the prescription refilled as soon as I could. "Same time tomorrow?"

She grinned. "It's a date."

"Don't say that too loud. Ana might hear you. We still need her to drive us back, remember?"

"Good point."

I felt like I was glowing. The exercise had helped to clear my head. No wonder I went to the gym so much. It was to keep my sanity, not the body I had in high school.

Marcy took the film out of the camera and palmed it. "There are a couple of one-hour photo places on Duval. When we get back, would you like to grab some breakfast while we get these developed?"

"Sounds great."

Ana held the deck panel open. Marcy and I dropped our gear into the hidden compartment. "What about you?" Marcy asked her. "Want to come with?"

She shook her head. "Can't. I have to work." She locked the panel and headed back to the captain's station. "But I do want you to have dinner with me tonight," she said, punching the button that raised the anchor.

"Both of us?" Marcy asked.

Ana looked from Marcy to me and back again. "If you want. Either way, I'll share and you'll listen."

It didn't take a rocket scientist to figure out what, or shall I say *who*, was going to be the topic of conversation.

Marcy and I headed below to shower and change.

"I didn't mean to get you in trouble," I said.

"You didn't," she said. "Ana's always on my case about something. That's another reason why we broke up. She had a tendency to act more like my mother than my girlfriend. That's okay every once in a while, but not twenty-four seven."

She gathered her things and headed to one of the guest staterooms to rid herself of the salty residue that had been left behind from our dip in the ocean, leaving me the master stateroom.

I rinsed my bathing suit in the sink and left it on the counter. I knew it wouldn't dry in the humid air, so I planned on wrapping it in the extra towel I'd brought and shoving it in my backpack when it was time to go. I stepped in the shower and turned on the spray, flinching a little as the water hit my skin. Despite my precautions, I'd gotten sunburned. Time would tell how badly.

I looked at my reflection in the mirror when I got out of the shower. My shoulders had burned a little, but they didn't hurt too badly. Yet. I moved closer to the mirror so I could carefully examine the body I had been walking around in for the past thirty-one years—the one that had seemed so unfamiliar to me less than twenty-four hours before. Now I remembered every line. Every curve.

The pale scar above my left knee was a remnant from a childhood spent climbing trees. Back then, my right side was markedly stronger than my left. As I tried to brace against the tree that was my obsession for the day, my left knee would always slip, scraping my skin painfully across the bark.

Much to her chagrin, my mother had been forced to make sure the hems of all my dresses fell below my knees so the world couldn't see how much of a tomboy I was. Like the world needed to see my knees to know that. Everything about me screamed, "This is not your average girly girl."

My father had instilled in both his children a love of sports and the outdoors. That love had never wavered, staying with Patrick and me throughout high school, college, and beyond. We followed the rising and falling fortunes of the Bulls, Bears, Blackhawks, and Cubs with almost fanatical obsession. My mother, accustomed to our delirium but immune to its effects, wondered why we took sports so seriously.

"They're just *games*," she'd say, standing in front of the TV. Funny how she always waited until the bottom of the ninth or the last minute of overtime to make her point. You'd almost be tempted to think she did it on purpose.

I smiled at the memory. As I got dressed, though, my good humor gradually faded. How long could I go on playing the aggrieved wife when I didn't know if I had earned the title?

When I got back to the house, I was going to have to do what I'd been putting off. I couldn't drag my feet any longer. I would have to watch the wedding video—and deal with whatever feelings that did or didn't arise as a result. I couldn't go on living in limbo. No matter how good a time I was having there.

Chapter Ten

Marcy and I dropped off the film at Photos in a Flash and headed to the Duval Beach Club for breakfast.

"You don't like to talk about yourself, do you?" Marcy asked as I dipped a piece of wheat toast in the soft center of my eggs over easy.

I tried to deflect her question. "Perhaps I'm not that interesting."

"Why don't you let me be the judge of that?"

I reached for my glass of orange juice in order to buy time. "Perhaps I'm afraid you'll judge me and find me unworthy."

"I doubt that."

"You're biased."

She blushed. "The whole wanting to get in your pants thing, you mean? Can you blame me?"

"I'm no great catch."

"Why don't you let me be the judge of that, too?" She had her teeth into the conversation. I couldn't shake her. She reached for the Heinz 57. "Just tell me one thing and I'll leave you alone."

"What's that?"

"Have you ever been with a woman before?"

I racked my semi-restored brain for the answer. "I don't think so," I eventually responded.

She arched one eyebrow. "You don't *think* so? Don't you know for sure?"

I tried to cover as best as I could without giving myself away. I remembered sleeping with a bunch of guys I didn't feel anything for, but I couldn't remember why I had subjected myself to that. Had I been trying to fit in or stand out? I remembered my father telling me I should be more selective with my choices and my mother telling me I should keep doing what I was doing. "You have to kiss a few frogs in order to find your prince," she had said. Was Jack my prince or just another frog? I felt the first stirrings of the vague unease that seemed to settle around me when I stumbled upon a subject I wasn't ready to fully explore.

"I've been in a couple of situations where I woke up the next day not knowing what the hell I had been thinking the night before—"

"When you would rather chew your arm off than disturb whoever you woke up next to? We've all been there at least once."

"With me, it was more than once."

"Were any of those times with a woman?" she asked, breaking her own rule about limiting herself to one question.

I reflected on the nights of drunken debauchery that had characterized my college years. I could remember making several walks of shame from the frat house with a couple of my sorority sisters in tow, but I couldn't remember making any similar pilgrimages from one of my sorority sister's rooms.

"That's actually something I've been thinking about since I met you," I said before I convinced myself not to.

Her ears perked up. "Really?"

"Yes, really. Not in an I-want-to-jump-your-bones kind of way. You might be ready to go there, but I'm not. I'm wondering if I could ever go there with a woman in general, not necessarily you in particular. I just met you, remember? We're still getting to know each other." And I was still getting to know myself.

"But I'm high on the list, right?" she asked.

I found her persistence charming, if a little off-putting. As an attorney, I was probably more accustomed to giving the third degree than receiving it.

"I can't tell if I'm attracted to you or to your attraction for me. I like being around you. I like the way you make me feel, even when you're making me feel uncomfortable. You're awfully good at that, by the way."

"So I've heard. I'm told I have no filter. I don't think that's a bad thing, but there are others who disagree with me."

"Am I right in assuming Ana's one of those people?"

"How'd you ever guess?" she asked with a wry smile. "But enough about me. Let's get back to you."

"What makes me such a fascinating topic of conversation?"

"Because I can't figure you out. I hate mysteries. I'm going to crack you if it's the last thing I do."

"That sounds painful."

"It does, doesn't it? Don't worry. I only bite on command. I won't clamp down until you tell me to."

"And if I don't?"

"Your loss."

She winked to cushion the blow. She reminded me of a colt that refused to walk because running was so much fun.

"How do you do it?" I asked.

"Do what?"

"Stay so upbeat all the time."

"You wouldn't say that if you'd seen me flipping burgers at a fast food restaurant in Podunk, Tennessee. There, I was the girl no one noticed. But when I got here, I opened up like a hothouse flower. I became the person I wanted to be instead of the one my family and so-called friends thought I should be. It's like I always say: sometimes you have to forget who you were to remember who you are."

Her words struck me with such force I could almost feel the blow. If I hadn't been sitting down, I might have hit the floor. What was it about them that had rung so true? Had I abandoned everyone and everything I knew in order to allow myself to become the person I was meant to be? To give myself the freedom to introduce myself to that person far from prying eyes? Marcy had come to Key West to find herself. I was doing the same thing. Literally as well as figuratively. The question was, would I be nearly as successful?

Marcy poured more ketchup on her house potatoes, then peered up at me. "Every time I look at you, you seem to be lost in thought. Did you come down here to think or to run and hide?"

"Probably a little bit of both."

"And which one are you doing more of?"

"That depends on what time of day you ask me."

She chewed her steak thoughtfully, debating whether to ask the question that was obviously on her mind. "When was the last time you talked to him?"

"Yesterday when I arrived."

"Did you talk about the subject at hand or did you dance around it?"

"I was standing in the middle of baggage claim at the airport, so it was kind of hard to get too personal. I asked him where we stand. He said we're—*he's* happy. *I* have my doubts."

"Is that why you're here with me?"

She made it sound like we were doing something illicit. All we were doing was having breakfast. I knew pork was bad for me, but it wasn't against the law for me to eat it. "I'm here with you because I enjoy your company. That isn't a crime, is it?"

"Not yet," she said. "Give me a couple of days. I'll see what I can do."

I wanted to tell her I thought she had learned her lesson with Ana about moving too fast, but doing so would have implied that I'd given serious consideration to sleeping with her. Yes, I'd thought about it, but only in passing. Sleeping with her didn't seem like the right thing to do. I thought it would confuse the issue, not make it clearer. If Jack and I were having problems, I didn't want to drag anyone else into it. That would only add fuel to any potential fire, and I already smelled smoke.

"Are you ready for tonight?" I asked.

The question took some of the wind out of her sails. "Ana's just going to lecture me and tell me that I'm making a mistake with you."

"Are you?"

"I can't answer that. You're the one who's holding all the cards. I'm just waiting for you to make your play."

"What if I don't?"

"I'll be disappointed, but I'll get over it. Eventually." She pushed her empty plate away. "I'm not stupid. I know you need a friend right now, not a lover. But when the time's right—when you're ready—I'd love to be both. If you tell me you just want to be friends, that's fine. If you tell me that you want to be more than that, that's fine, too. Just pick one and stick with it. Don't waffle back and forth."

"Is that what you think I'm doing now?"

"I don't know what you're doing now," she said. "On the plus side, I don't think you do, either."

"So what do we do in the meantime?"

"You figure things out; I wait for that to happen."

I wiped my mouth with my napkin and tossed the napkin onto my empty plate. "Pardon me, but you don't seem like a patient person."

"I didn't say I'd be waiting patiently. Believe me, I'll be trying to help you along as best I can."

"How do you plan on doing that?" She slowly unspooled a smile filled with wicked promise. She opened her mouth to speak, but I stopped her before she could. "On second thought, don't answer that."

She tossed a tip onto the table for the waitress. "Since I kept you from your grocery shopping, the least I can do is take you by the store. The Circle K is five blocks from here. I can drop you off or hang around. Which would you prefer?"

"I'd love the company, but I don't want to keep you from anything."

"You won't be. I don't work for any of the tour companies. I'm an independent operator. That means I have the luxury of setting my own hours. If I want to work, I do. If I don't, I don't. Right now, I don't. I'd rather be with you. If that's okay."

Suddenly I felt like I was in over my head. There was nothing wrong with a little harmless flirting, but what we were doing no longer felt harmless. Marcy had made it clear that she could develop feelings for me if I gave her half a chance, but I couldn't make such an offer to her—or anyone else—until I gave myself one.

Chapter Eleven

Expecting company?" Marcy asked, cutting the engine on the scooter.

"No." I followed her line of sight. A car was parked in front of my vacation house. The black Toyota Camry had Florida plates and a "KW" sticker on the back window, marking it as a local vehicle. "I'm sure it's one of the neighbors," I said. "His driveway's probably blocked so he borrowed mine. That's cool."

I reached for one of the two grocery bags. Marcy grabbed the other. The pictures were in my backpack. We had ordered double prints so each of us could have copies. We hadn't pored through them when we picked them up—too eager to put the groceries away and crack open a couple of cold beers. Thinking I would need plenty of alcohol to get me through my afternoon chore, I had bought a six-pack of Heineken and a bottle of Wild Turkey.

Marcy and I headed up the sidewalk, ready to examine the photos of our underwater expedition. I felt like Jacques Cousteau minus the cute little hat. Until I saw that the front door was ajar. Then all I felt was fear. I touched Marcy's arm for support.

We froze in shock, uncertain whether to venture into the house or run next door to call 911.

"Are you sure you're not expecting company?" she asked.

"Positive."

We didn't hear any sounds from inside. Brave or crazy or both, we cautiously climbed the steps.

The door swung open. A tall dark-haired man dressed like Tiger Woods on a Sunday afternoon—red polo shirt and black golf pants—stood in the doorway.

Marcy stepped in front of me protectively. "Who the fuck are you?" she barked at him.

I answered for him. "My husband."

CHAPTER TWELVE

"Jack, what are you doing here?" I asked.

"I was worried about you," he said matter-of-factly. When he bent to kiss me, I offered him my cheek instead of my lips. "You sounded so distant on the phone that I had to come see you. I cleared my schedule for the rest of the week and hopped the first plane I could."

"Are you going to be here that long?" I couldn't imagine living in close quarters with someone I barely knew—even if I did bear his last name.

"Unless you have any objections."

I had plenty, but how was I supposed to raise them?

He took the grocery bag out of my arms and turned to Marcy. He stuck out his hand. "Jack Stanton. Who might you be?"

"A friend of your wife's." She shook his hand, then cast a withering glance at me as Jack possessively draped his left arm across my shoulders. "Or at least I thought I was."

Unable to face the unspoken accusations in her eyes, I turned to Jack. "You didn't have to come," I told him. "I'm fine."

He chucked me under my chin. "Maybe I wanted to see it for myself."

Marcy thrust the other bag of groceries toward me. "You

look like you're in good hands," she said. "I'm going to take off."

"Wait!" I called after her as she rushed down the stairs. I handed Jack the groceries and dug around in my backpack for the extra set of prints. "You almost forgot your pictures."

"Right," she said without much enthusiasm. "Wouldn't want to forget those." She slid the photos into her back pocket without looking at them.

Jack went inside the house, presumably to put the groceries away. I used the respite to apologize to Marcy. Or try to. "I'm sorry. I didn't know he was going to be here."

"It doesn't matter. Whether he's here or in Chicago, it doesn't change the fact that you lied to me."

"About what?" I grabbed her arm, but she pulled away.

"About everything. If you two are so unhappy, why did you greet him with open arms?"

"If that's what you think you saw, you need to have your eyes examined."

"Why are we even arguing about this, anyway? You're *married*, remember?" she said, reminding both of us of something we seemed to have momentarily forgotten. She started the scooter. "Go play with your husband. I've got better things to do than wait around for you to decide if you're actually interested in me or if you're just another bi-curious straight girl."

Just as they had in the restaurant, her words found their mark. This time they hit me even harder. I actually staggered a little. What she said had an air of familiarity I could neither pinpoint nor dismiss.

"I am being as honest with you as I know how," I said, blocking her escape route. "What do you want from me?"

She glared at me, her eyes filled with equal parts hurt and anger. "Apparently something you're not ready to give."

She was right and I knew it, so I didn't try to argue with her. She had tried to draw me out, but I had deflected all of her questions. When I'd had the chance to come clean, I had chosen to keep my secret. My actions might have ended our friendship before it had barely begun.

I stepped aside and Marcy sped away. I watched her until she disappeared around the corner. Then I headed back inside. I found Jack in the kitchen. The medical encyclopedia lay open on the banquette. Had he glanced at it and seen what I'd been reading or had he been too busy with the groceries? Not taking any chances, I closed the book while his back was turned.

"Where's your friend?" he asked, bending to put the salad mix in the crisper.

"She had to go to work."

"Oh?" He cribbed one of the fresh strawberries before putting the carton in the refrigerator. "What does she do?"

"She drives a pedi-cab," I said while he popped the cap on two of the Heinekens. He handed me one and kept one for himself.

"That sounds strenuous. Especially considering how hot and humid it gets down here during the summer. What's her name again?"

"It's Marcy," I said, wishing he'd change the subject.

"How did you meet her?"

"Walking down the street," I offered lamely. Unable to remember what kind of relationship we had, I didn't know how to relate to him. I had hoped I wouldn't have to until I was myself again. Hadn't the phone call been enough to put his mind at ease?

He wriggled his eyebrows at me. "Back to that again, are you?"

"You said you didn't mind if I went back to work. Why shouldn't I have a go at the world's oldest profession?"

He laughed around the mouth of his beer bottle. "How's your new job working out for you?"

"It's slow going right now. I'll let you know after I build up a client base."

"Do I have to stand in line for your services or will I be afforded special privileges?" His voice was a seductive murmur.

I was afraid he'd ask a question along those lines. When I saw him standing in the doorway, the first thought that had run through my mind was *What do I do if he asks for sex?* I couldn't say no without an explanation, but how could I say yes? I hadn't reclaimed my memories of him so I felt like we were meeting for the first time. The "new" me wasn't into sex with strangers and that's what he was to me—a stranger.

"I'll check my schedule and get back to you."

"You do that," he said, laughing again. He dipped into the bag of potato chips I'd bought.

"Did they not feed you on the plane or are you just a bottomless pit today?"

He grinned but didn't put down the chips. "This is why you don't allow me in the kitchen when you're unpacking groceries. I was going to take you to lunch today, but you look satiated. In more ways than one, I might add. You look more relaxed than I've seen you in weeks. What have you been doing all morning?"

"Marcy and I went snorkeling at the reef."

I pulled out the pictures to back up my story. Jack latched on to the first shot Marcy had taken, the one of me being greeted by a fishy welcoming committee. "This is a good picture of you. You look like The Little Mermaid." He rifled through a few more pictures. "Why haven't we ever done this?"

"I don't know," I said with a shrug as I gathered the scattered photos. "Timing, I guess."

"Maybe tomorrow?"

I wanted to make another trip out to the reef, but venturing there with someone other than Marcy or Ana would have felt somehow dishonest. In order to make the trip with Jack, I would have to use another charter company. "I'll see what I can do."

He pulled me into his arms for a crushing hug and a delayed hello kiss that was only slightly less bruising. "God, I missed you."

"I haven't been gone that long." The arms around me were strong and sure. I tried to recall how I was supposed to feel when I was in them.

Jack was as handsome in person as he was in the picture I'd found in my wallet. Despite being a bit presumptuous, he seemed to be a genuinely nice guy. I should have been overjoyed to discover that a man that perfect belonged to me. Instead, I was wondering why I didn't feel a spark between us. My heart should have skipped a beat when I'd seen him, not stopped altogether.

He'd just arrived and I couldn't wait for him to leave.

He's your husband, I reminded myself. *Just relax and let it happen*.

"Last night was the first night we've spent apart since we got married," he said. "I didn't handle it very well." He laced his fingers around my waist and pressed his hips against mine. His semi-erection poked against my stomach. "Have you gone to your favorite place yet?"

Assuming he meant Sloppy Joe's, I tried to think of an appropriate response. "I didn't want to go without you."

He frowned and I wondered if I'd given myself away. "That's never stopped you before. You make a beeline for that place every time you come down here. The only company you require there is Mr. Hemingway's, not Dr. Stanton's." He kissed me on my forehead and let me go. I was grateful for the reprieve. The bulge pressing against my navel was distracting. "You know something?" he said, taking another sip of his beer. "I think your friend the pedi-cab driver would be perfect for Jennifer. But you already knew that, didn't you?"

"What do you mean?" I asked, trying not to appear as shocked as I felt. He made it sound like Jennifer was into women. Nothing I had seen or heard in the previous two days had led me in that direction. If Jennifer were gay, why was she living with Marcus? Was he not, as I'd assumed, her husband? Was he simply what he'd claimed to be when I'd talked to him on the phone—a sidekick? A roommate and nothing more?

I quickly re-examined the videotaped images I'd seen the night before. I thought back to the smile Jennifer and Marcus had shared. They had smiled at each other not like they were the only two people in the room, but the only two people *like them*. And when I'd teased Jennifer about her and Patrick having feelings for each other, I'd known then why that wasn't the case. He might have had feelings for her, but she hadn't felt the same way.

Why had I blocked out something so important? What other secrets had I forgotten? What else was I supposed to know?

"You more than anyone knows how much Jennifer loves the athletic type," Jack said. "Your new friend definitely fits the bill. Not that I was looking."

"No, heaven forbid," I said, pretending to be jealous. I was so accomplished at doing what was expected of me that I wondered how good I was at doing what came naturally.

"Have you talked to her?"

"Who?" I didn't know if he meant my old friend or my new one.

"Jen."

I borrowed one of Marcus's lines in order to save my ass. "She's off saving the world again. I couldn't get through to her."

"I can't believe she agreed to another stint so soon after the last one. I thought she would have taken some time to get all that madness out of her head before she subjected herself to another round of it. She was home only a week, if that long. Where is she this time? She's not back in the Sudan, is she?"

"I'm not sure," I said. Was I supposed to know?

Jack nodded sympathetically. "I have a couple of contacts with Doctors Without Borders. I could give one of them a call and find out. Not that it would make much difference—one war is as deadly as another once the bullets start flying—but I'm sure it would ease your mind to know exactly where she is. I remember how upset you were when she volunteered to go to Liberia after the violence there began to spin out of control. You barely slept for almost a week. Is that why you're here now, so you can walk the floor at night without keeping me awake?"

It sounded like a reasonable explanation as any. "You found me out."

"She'll be fine," he said. "She always is. Remember her motto? 'I might not know much, but one thing I know how to do is stay alive.'"

Jennifer was as lost to me as Jack was, but I somehow felt her absence more. Probably because I had seen how happy and how close we used to be. Dancing goofily in our prom dresses. Ganging up on my brother. We didn't just look like sisters. We had acted like them as well.

"What am I supposed to do if she forgets how to stay alive?" I asked.

"She won't." Jack held my face in his hands and peered into my eyes. "Why don't you ever worry about me like that?"

"Have you ever given me reason to?"

I doubted it. He seemed too staid to do anything that would cause me to lose sleep over him. He would be home when he said he would. He would call if he had to work late. He wouldn't forget birthdays or anniversaries. He was a romance novelist's dream. So why didn't he feel like mine?

"I am the antithesis of all those bad boys you dated in high school and college," he said. "I try to be as dull and boring as possible. It's why you married me, isn't it? That and the fact that I'm hung like a horse."

"If you say so."

Why *had* I married him? Had it been love at first sight or had friendship blossomed into more? Had he swept me off my feet or had I needed convincing? Had he chased me or had I gone after him?

"Tell me our story."

"Don't you remember it?" He asked the question so seriously that I thought he might finally be on to me.

"I want to make sure that *you* do."

"If you're putting me on the spot after less than two years, I can't imagine what you're going to do after fifty."

"More of the same, only worse."

Despite his mild protest, he granted my request. We made ourselves comfortable on the couch and he told me how we came to be.

"I suppose you could say Jennifer is the reason we're together. She and I fought tooth-and-nail all through med school to see who could get the best grades and the best girls. If she and I weren't so competitive, I never would have met you," he said, still nursing his beer. Out of sorts, I was already on my second. "My shift was over. I should have been on my way home. With nothing better to do, I decided to challenge Jennifer to a little one-on-one."

An image of a basketball court with faded paint and rotting nets popped into my head, but I didn't know if it was the one from Jack's story or something I'd seen on TV. Still, I felt a spark of hope. Perhaps Jack was the missing link. The piece of the puzzle I needed to make the rest fall into place.

"She and I were in the middle of the game when you showed up to take her out for your regular Friday let-me-tell-you-what-a-shitty-week-I-had get-together," Jack continued. "Before that night, I had come close to beating her—if losing by single digits instead of double counts as close—but I had never taken a game off of her. I looked so hapless that night I managed to make you feel sorry for me. You gave me some pointers on my form and my defense. With your help, I was finally able to take her down. When my final shot swished through the net, I think you celebrated even more than I did."

He chuckled at the memory.

"Jennifer was so angry with you for 'turning on her,' as she put it, that she bailed on dinner. You, however, graciously allowed me to serve as her stand-in. I spent the next two hours trying to convince you not to judge me solely on my athletic ability—or lack thereof. It must have worked because you agreed to see me again. We moved in together three months later. Six months after that, we were married. I've never been certain if you said yes to me or to the opportunity to watch eighty-one free Cubs games from the roof of my apartment building. You said it was me, but I have my doubts."

"Let me ease your mind," I said. "It was the Cubs."

He nodded as if he'd been expecting the joke. My memory might have been faulty, but my personality seemed to be intact. Despite everything, I was still the same person.

I had hoped Jack's retelling of our story would prompt a flood of memories like the home videos had the night before. When he finished, I didn't know anything other than what he'd told me. He felt like a guy I was chatting amiably with while killing time in an airport bar, not the man I'd promised to spend the rest of my life with.

"Did I leave anything out?" he asked.

Plenty. When was the first time we slept together? When was the last? What had happened in the past few days—the past few *weeks*—to make me want to forget who I was? Why couldn't I remember anything about Jennifer, the woman I'd declared my "best friend for life"? Why couldn't I remember anything about him or our life together?

"No, I think you covered everything."

His right hand slid up my thigh. The action reawakened something in me that had stirred to life when I was with Marcy: an overwhelming need for human contact. I wanted to connect with someone. Someone tangible, not frozen in time on a videotape.

I was tired of wandering aimlessly. I wanted my life back. All of it, not just the bits and pieces. I wanted to remember the good times as well as the bad.

Ready to face whatever I was running from, I tried a little shock therapy.

Straddling Jack's lap, I cupped a hand over his crotch to check the state of his arousal. He groaned, then ground his hips against my palm.

I unzipped his fly and reached inside to free his insistent member. He pulled my shorts and underwear down and guided me onto his shaft. I pulled his shirt over his head and tossed it on the floor. I raked my nails across his back, bit into his shoulder. Clutching at him, I pulled him deeper inside me.

"Come on," I said. "Make me feel it. Make me remember."

My hips thrust wildly. He tried to keep pace—to match my rhythm—but I was like a woman possessed.

"Jesus, Syd," he gasped. "What's gotten into you? You're like a different person."

I was tantalizingly close to the edge, but I couldn't quite make it to the other side. I couldn't concentrate with him babbling about my performance.

I covered his mouth with my hand. "Shh," I said. "Don't talk."

He drew one of my fingers into his mouth and I felt a sense of déjà vu. I had been in that situation before. The build-up. The anticipation. The loss of control. I had felt those sensations before—but not with him. Never with him. Or any of my other partners. Only with—

Everything stopped.

Jack came, grunting as if I'd punched him in the gut.

He kissed me as he fought to catch his breath. "You were right," he said, resting his head on my chest to make the moment last. "Whatever you're working through *doesn't* have anything to do with us. That was unbelievable. Definitely worth waiting five months for."

I looked down at him. "Five *months*? Has it been that long since we were together?"

He combed his mussed hair with his fingers. "We used to go at it like rabbits before we said 'I do.' After we got back from our honeymoon, life started getting in the way, and before we knew it we were, for lack of a better term, two ships passing in the night. When I was coming from work, you were heading to it and vice versa. You were too busy trying to make partner to notice, but I certainly did. If we made love once or twice a month, I considered myself lucky. But it's been months since you let me touch you. Four months, three weeks, and six days, to be exact."

I climbed off his lap. "Why don't you give me the minutes and seconds while you're at it?"

I was irritated with myself for leaving him twisting in the wind for so long and with him for allowing me to get away with it. I was tempted to call him an enabler, but it wasn't his fault I was too much of a coward to face whatever was bothering me. Instead of owning up to my issues, I had buried them so deeply that I could no longer reach them. Or had that been the point?

"Why is sex such a sore subject for you?" he asked. "You shut down every time I bring it up, but lately, it's even worse. Ever since the firm assigned you to the Slasher case, you've refused to let anyone get too close, me included. The armchair psychiatrist in me is tempted to say you're identifying too much with one of the principals in the case."

"Do you think I'm a victim or a defendant?" I didn't appreciate being compared to either.

He smiled wanly. "You tell me."

Why would I relate to anyone in a case as gruesome as the Subway Slasher's? Granted, I didn't know all the details, but even the name sounded grisly. If I had known I'd been involved in the case, I would have asked the guy on the flight from Chicago if I could have borrowed his copy of the *Tribune* when he was done with it so I could have seen what I was a part of.

Jack held up his hands in surrender. "Babe, I don't want to fight with you. Let me have my moment. Today is the first time in a long time that you didn't make me feel like you consented to sex simply as a favor to me. It felt like you were enjoying yourself, not fulfilling a marital obligation."

I didn't have the heart to tell him otherwise. I had been attempting to fill a need, but not the one he had in mind.

I had hoped sleeping with him would bring us closer together. Instead, it had driven us even further apart, leaving me with more questions than answers. Why was it taking me so long to figure things out? And why had making love with my husband felt like a betrayal? If he was the person I had committed myself to, body and soul, why did I feel like those things belonged to someone else?

CHAPTER THIRTEEN

Jack called dibs on the shower. While he was gone, I forced myself to perform the task I had been avoiding. It was time for me to face my fears. All of them.

I retrieved the wedding video and slid it into the VCR. "Here goes nothing," I said and pressed Play.

Shot from a camera mounted in the rear of the church, the video was filmed by a professional. What it made up for in quality, it lacked in charm. The prom night video—filmed by my brother, my father, and my best friend—had captured a slice of my life, shaky images and all. The wedding video, by contrast, was more like a documentary with no point of view. Its only objective was to chronicle, not illuminate.

I watched as guests were ushered in and took their seats. Instead of speaking in reverent whispers, they were nearly as rowdy as a European soccer crowd. The din subsided only when the ushers began escorting first my grandmother, then Jack's, down the aisle.

The processional music began. Ushers saw my mother, then Jack's, to their seats. My mother, resplendent in a beaded beige dress, was beaming like it was her wedding day. Jack's mother, on the other hand, looked like she'd been sucking on an exceptionally sour lemon. Seeing her again reminded me of her disdain for me. I had bent over backwards to please her, but nothing I had done had worked. In her eyes, I would never be good enough for her son.

Maybe she was right.

A side door opened. Reverend William Hughes entered the room, followed by Jack and his best man/younger brother Jimmy. Jack looked nervous. Jimmy looked like he couldn't wait to find the nearest bar—or had spent too much time in one the night before. The four groomsmen who trailed behind him—my brother included—seemed to be in similarly rough shape.

At the altar, Jimmy fiddled with his bow tie until a sharp look from Jack made him stop. Then everyone turned to watch the bridesmaids enter.

My sister-in-law Kristin began the slow parade. I recognized her right away. The same was true for the four women who followed her: two of my former sorority sisters from college, my workout partner from the gym, and Jennifer's girlfriend Natalie Zabriskie. Each woman's hair was styled in similar fashion—upswept and held in place by a spray of baby's breath. All five were dressed in identical black satin gowns held up by the thinnest of spaghetti straps. Sheer red scarves draped across their shoulders and trailing down their backs provided a dash of color. The scarlet accessory matched the bouquet of roses in their hands.

My nephew Kris was the ring bearer. The flower girl accompanying him down the aisle was a beautiful little redhead from his second grade class. I remembered Kris taking great delight in telling everyone she was his girlfriend. She, on the other hand, hadn't gotten the memo. She had liked the attention he paid her, but she had shied away every time he had tried to kiss her. "Boys are icky," she had eloquently explained.

Jennifer, my maid of honor, appeared next on the screen.

She had the same dress and hairstyle as the rest of my bridesmaids, but her bouquet was larger, denoting her higher rank in the bridal party.

I moved closer to the TV screen, expecting realization to wash over me like a tidal wave, but Jennifer remained maddeningly out of reach.

She walked with her head up and her shoulders square, as if she were balancing an invisible book on her noggin. She took her place next to Reverend Hughes and turned toward the back of the church. Her smile seemed a little off. It looked brave, not genuine. As if she were pretending to be happy instead of actually enjoying the moment. I had been too nervous to notice it at the time, but hindsight's twenty-twenty.

The organist pounded out the opening strains of the wedding march. All the guests rose as one and turned to await my grand entrance. Watching the tape, I was filled with as much anticipation as they were—and I was waiting to see myself.

My face hidden by a white lace veil, I walked down the aisle on my father's arm. He stood next to me at the altar while Jennifer bent to straighten my train.

Reverend Hughes said a few words to welcome everyone and to reiterate the reason we were there. He followed up with a lengthy prayer that left our souls lifted and our necks sore. I could see several guests rubbing theirs after Reverend Hughes said *Amen*.

After the congregation sang "Amazing Grace," the "official" part of the ceremony began.

Reverend Hughes asked, "Who gives this woman in marriage?"

Dad replied, "Her mother and I do." Then he kissed me on the cheek, symbolically handed me off to Jack, and joined my mother in the front row.

Jack and I exchanged vows without interruption—no one

stood when Reverend Hughes uttered the always dramatic "Speak now or forever hold your peace." I expected Patrick or Jennifer to do or say something to break the tension, but they remained mute. He was too wobbly from the night before; she was too concerned with doing her job as my maid of honor. I could almost see her counting items off her mental checklist.

"Walk in heels without busting your ass. Check. Slowly turn and smile. Check. Send supportive vibes to best friend while she attempts to duplicate your feat of walking without tripping. Check. Adjust train. Check. Take bouquet. Check. Make Reverend Hughes hurry things along so you can get out of this dress and have a beer. Check."

The rest of the ceremony was uneventful. Nothing out of the ordinary. I kept waiting for an "aha" moment when everything would suddenly make sense.

When Jack kissed me, his new bride, a little too long, Reverend Hughes cracked, "Save some for the honeymoon, son." His comment provoked a laugh from the congregation, who burst into applause when Reverend Hughes introduced Jack and me as Dr. and Mrs. John J. Stanton.

As we faced our friends and now-blended families, Jack looked delirious with happiness; I looked, to be honest, relieved. The camera followed Jack and me as we headed out of the church before it panned back to catch the attendants' departures. Jennifer and Jimmy were the first to leave. Even though she was dressed for a wedding, Jennifer looked like she was attending a funeral. I zoomed in on her grim, unsmiling face and hit the pause button. I pressed my hand against the screen.

Jennifer. My soul mate. The love of my life.

I remembered.

How could I forget?

She told me she was gay when we were in the ninth grade. She had a crush on the most popular girl in school—Rachel Nicholson, the captain of the cheerleading squad—but she told only me. I kept her secret, though that didn't stop other people from guessing it. Something in her eyes gave her away. Truly the mirrors to her soul, they were unable to hide what she was feeling. They still are.

At the time she came out to me, I was so naïve I barely knew what the word *lesbian* meant, but I envied her. I wanted to be as comfortable in my own skin as she was. To be so young but so certain about who and what I wanted.

Back then, I had been too busy wondering what people thought of me to just be myself. Instead, I had tried on and discarded personas as if I were shopping for jeans at the mall. None of them had been a perfect fit so I had picked the one I thought I could grow into: the type-A overachiever. I had set nearly impossible goals and hadn't stopped until I reached them. When I did, I had set the bar even higher. All so I wouldn't have to face the image and esteem issues that had set in when I was fifteen. That was the year I had developed an acne condition so serious it had earned me the odious nickname Pizza Face.

"You're beautiful," Jennifer used to tell me even when my forehead looked like a slice of double-stuffed pepperoni. "When you're older, you'll look back on all this and laugh. You'll show up for the class reunion happy and successful and supermodel gorgeous and all those assholes that are being jerks to you now will be eating their hearts out."

I hadn't believed her, of course. I tended to dwell on negative comments and ignore positive ones. I guess not much had changed from high school to now.

Even though Jennifer was into girls and I was into guys,

it hadn't stopped us from being friends. But it had tested our bond. She had listened attentively while I told her all about my latest adventure in the backseat of some guy's car. When it was her turn to share, I hadn't paid her the same courtesy. I didn't want to hear her talk about Frenching a girl or getting to second base.

I was jealous of her girlfriends. Not them personally. I didn't find fault with them as *people*. I didn't like the *idea* of them. Time Jennifer spent with them was time she spent away from me. I resented them for taking her away from me. I hadn't known how to put that into words. If I had, perhaps I wouldn't have wasted so much time feeling sorry for myself and spent more time being a better friend. I made up for it later—I gave her my shoulder to cry on during senior year when she broke up with her first serious girlfriend—but I would do anything to get back the years in between.

Out of respect for her parents, Jennifer had kept her burgeoning sexuality under wraps until she got to college. In high school, Marcus was her beard—and she was his. They had helped each other fulfill society's expectations of what was "normal" while, at the same time, remaining true to themselves. They had come bursting out of their respective closets after they joined a student-run GLBT group on campus in Champaign, but their friendship had endured. I had often wondered if she were closer to him than to me.

"You and he have something in common that you and I don't," I'd tell her.

"Are you sure?" she'd retort. I'd thought she was kidding. My sexuality was a constant topic of debate for her friends. So much so that it became a joke for us. When I went to parties with her, we used to call them recruiting trips.

The "recruiters" had come calling in high school. Because I was a good athlete—I lettered in soccer and basketball—and because Jennifer and I were so close—we spent every waking moment together—most of her friends had assumed I was gay. A few of them had hit on me. I hadn't been offended, but I hadn't accepted any of their proposals.

My "rampant heterosexuality" was a cover, they had said. They had asked me what I was compensating for. I hadn't thought I was compensating for anything. I had thought I was just having fun. Looking for my prince. Who knew that what I really wanted was a princess?

I had listened respectfully when my father had given me the old "men won't buy the cow if they can get the milk for free" speech, but it had felt like he'd been secretly pleased to be delivering that lecture instead of the one that began "So what's this I hear about you having feelings for other girls?"

I didn't have feelings for other girls. I had feelings for one girl: Jennifer. Except by the time I realized it, it was too late to do anything about it. I was married to Jack and she was off in the middle of a civil war.

My parents adored Jennifer and they said they didn't have any issues with her sexual preferences, but they made it clear that what was okay for her was not okay for me.

"You don't want to be like your cousin Tommy, do you?" my mother had once asked, referring to a distant relative we saw once a year, if that.

My cousin Tommy had a great job, a fabulous house, and a gorgeous boyfriend. Why wouldn't I want to be like him?

The message I had garnered from my mother's rambling explanation was this: even though Tommy seemed to be happy and well-adjusted, I was supposed to pity him because his happiness wasn't "real." By whose definition? I wish I had been brave enough to ask the question but, though we were urged to stand up for ourselves, Patrick and I weren't encouraged to second-guess our parents.

I had said yes to Jack's proposal because I loved him, not because of his apartment's prime vantage point across from Wrigley Field. But, as I often teased, that had helped seal the deal.

The whining of the hair dryer in the bathroom snapped me out of my reverie. Jack was out of the shower. I didn't have much time.

I restarted the video and skipped ahead to the reception. Watching myself dance with my father put a lump in my throat the same way it had that day. Back then I had been overjoyed to make him so proud of me. Nineteen months later, I feared what his reaction would be when I told him that day had been a mistake. He'd still love me. Of that, I was certain. What I wanted was his approval. I didn't know if he would grant it.

At the reception, the lobster dinner was frequently interrupted by the sound of silverware tinkling against crystal water glasses—the traditional sign that the new bride and groom should stop what they were doing to kiss. It was fun the first five or six times. The last fifteen or twenty were a bit tiresome.

Where was Reverend Hughes and his "save some for the honeymoon" when I needed him? Oh, yes. Hiding behind the five-foot floral arrangement in the middle of the gift table so he could quaff champagne without being seen.

One person after another stood up to make toasts.

Patrick's toast was funny. Recounting the prom night story, he warned Jack to never take me by surprise. "But if you feel you must," he said, "duck fast because she's got a wicked left hand."

I drew a laugh by pretending to draw back as if to punch him. Then I kissed him and gave him a hug. "Thank you, big brother," I whispered in his ear. "I love you."

"I love you, too, sis," he replied. The big lug actually teared up on me. Like most siblings, we fought like cats and dogs but had each other's backs when it counted.

Jack's father's toast was gracious. "I have always wanted a daughter," he said, raising his glass in my direction. "Now I can finally say I have one. Welcome to the family, Sydney. I hope you feel as welcome in ours as you do your own."

He gave me a crushing hug. My new mother-in-law didn't follow suit. When she had hugged me, I had barely felt the pressure. She would ratchet that up in due time.

My father's toast was touching. "I became a parent the day my kids were born. I became a grandfather the day my son introduced me to his son. I didn't become a father until today, when I saw my daughter get married. Jack, you're a good man. I'm happy to have you in my daughter's life—and in mine. Congratulations, you two. May your worst day together be ten times better than my best."

He and my mother drew Jack and me into their arms. I had cried like a baby, makeup running everywhere. I'm surprised I didn't end up looking like a wet raccoon in any of the pictures. I looked dazed in most of them, but that was nothing new.

Unnerved by either the occasion or by having to follow something so heartfelt, Jimmy hemmed and hawed through his speech. He dropped more *um*'s, *uh*'s, and *ah*'s than Jonathan Demme had when he accepted his Oscar as Best Director for *The Silence of the Lambs*. I was so embarrassed for him that I hit fast forward until he was done.

Jennifer was last to speak. Before she took the microphone, she quickly downed a glass of champagne for fortification.

"When you write," she began, "you're supposed to write what you know. When you speak, you're supposed to speak from the heart. Since I hate to write and I can't stand public speaking, I'm not quite sure which way I'm supposed to go. For those of you who know me, I'm sure that doesn't come as much of a surprise."

Her captive audience laughed over their chocolate éclairs.

"Sydney has been my best friend for as long as I can remember," Jennifer continued. "We've been through more together than any two people have a right to. Whenever anything good happens in my life, she's the one I want to share it with. Whenever anything bad happens, she's the one who makes me feel better. She knows what I'm going to say even before I do. This is one time I think I'm going to catch her by surprise."

She paused dramatically while the crowd *ooh*ed in anticipation.

"Because I'm going to ignore her completely. Jack, this message is for you," she said, putting him on the spot instead. "Take care of her even when she says she doesn't need you to. Listen to her even when what she's saying is unspoken. Love her no matter what. Do these three things and we won't have a problem, will we, Doctor?"

"No, ma'am," he obediently replied.

"Uh-oh, Jack," a heckler called out. "Looks like you've got two wives instead of one."

"Better than three," Jack shot back.

His sarcastic comeback ingratiated him with the men but alienated him from the women, including the members of his fan club—the half-dozen nurses from the hospital who occupied a table near the dais. They pelted Jack with the souvenir miniature silver wedding bells that had been handed out to each guest.

"Looks like someone won't be getting any tonight," Jennifer joked. "I guess my job here's done."

I stopped the tape. I had seen enough to make me remember the rest. Jack and I had visited each table to thank our guests for coming, then we had paused to cut the four-tier Italian cream wedding cake. Accompanied by much wolf whistling, Jack had slid the blue garter off my leg. Jimmy had out leaped the other single men to claim the prize. The scrum for my wedding bouquet had threatened to turn into an all-out brawl. A few hours before, my bachelorette party had nearly degenerated into chaos as well.

The night before the wedding, Jennifer and Natalie had taken me to T's, one of their favorite lesbian hangouts. To prevent me from having a final fling or hoping that I would have one, neither would say. Whatever their reasons, the surroundings had put a whole new spin on the party games, let me tell you. Especially when the object of one of the games was for me to collect as many kisses from perfect strangers as I could.

At the party, I'd downed several shots of tequila on a half-empty stomach, but I'd managed to remain upright. Even when Natalie had done her best to floor me. She'd been cool to me all night. When I'd asked her why, she'd steered me to a quiet corner and lit into me.

"I'm going to tell you what your best friend won't," she'd said. (I hate when people begin sentences that way.) "Jen's leaving and it's all your fault."

"Leaving?" I hadn't known if she'd meant Jennifer was leaving town or leaving her. Jennifer hadn't mentioned either scenario to me. "What do you mean she's leaving?"

"She wants to get as far away from you as possible. Not that I blame her."

"Where's she going?"

"Darfur."

A knot had immediately formed in the pit of my stomach.

Jennifer couldn't have picked a worse place if she had tried. Darfur was a simmering cauldron of violence that could boil over at any time.

"If something happens to her," Natalie had said, "I'll never forgive you."

"If something happened to her, I'd never forgive myself, but I don't think her decision has anything to do with me. She's always running off to one natural disaster or another. Even though this one is man-made, the concept remains the same."

"Open your eyes, Syd," Natalie had snapped. "Darfur's an excuse, not a destination. She's leaving because she's in love with you. She always has been. Why do you think she's leaving next week? Because she'd rather live in hell than watch you with Jack. I don't know what she sees in you. Whenever I look at you, all I can do is ask myself how such an intelligent woman can make such foolish choices. This isn't the fifties. You don't have to hide behind a man. With a law degree in your pocket, you could easily support yourself if you wanted to. Jennifer would throw me over for you in a heartbeat if she thought you could ever come to terms with who you are, but you're too much of a closet case to ever let that happen."

"Whoa, hold on. First of all, I'm not a closet case. Second, there are three women Jen's always said she would never fall for: a straight woman, a married woman, and her best friend. I'm all three."

Natalie had rolled her eyes so hard she had nearly fallen asleep standing up. "Not quite."

"Okay, so I'm not married yet. Two out of three ain't bad."

I had tried to use levity to lighten the mood, but Natalie hadn't been able to find any humor in the situation.

"You might want to crunch those numbers again. Or do

you have so much internalized homophobia that you can't think straight? Pun intended."

I had known where she was going but I hadn't wanted to go there with her. "You think I'm... Does Jennifer think I'm..."

"I'm not going to put words in your mouth, Syd. But until you can say the words, I'm not having this conversation with you."

She had tried to walk away and I had tried to stop her. Jennifer had separated us before our war of words could turn physical.

"This side of the room is much too serious," she said. "In case you've forgotten, this is supposed to be a party."

She had bought a round of tequila shots as a peace offering, but the truce had proven to be only temporary. Relations between Natalie and me had remained frosty at best.

I was roaring drunk by the end of the night. Jennifer had taken me home and poured me into bed. When she had tried to excuse herself to head to Natalie's apartment for some "late-night aerobics," I had talked her out of it.

"We both know she's pissed at you right now," I had slurred, "so why don't you give her a little more time to cool off?"

"Good idea." She had lain next to me on the bed, sliding her pillow close to mine as if we were going to spend the rest of the night sharing secrets. We had hinted around them instead, neither of us quite able to trust the other with the complete truth. She was in love with me and couldn't tell me; I was concerned for her safety but didn't want my fears to be a distraction for her.

"When were you going to tell me about Darfur?"

"You've read the paper. You've seen the news. I shouldn't have to tell you what's going on over there."

I had punched her lightly on the shoulder so she could realize I was serious. "Okay, smartass, when were you going to tell me that you'd be in the middle of it?"

"This weekend is supposed to be about you, not me."

"So you were going to let me come home from my honeymoon to find you gone?"

"Of course not, but—"

"Natalie says I'm the reason you're leaving. Is that true?"

"Unless you joined the militia while my back was turned, you're not the reason I'm needed over there."

It had been a hedge but I had let her get away with it because I had been more concerned with her answer to my follow-up question.

"She also says you're in love with me."

"She says a lot of things when she's drinking tequila. *In vino veritas.* Truth is in the wine. Isn't that how the saying goes? There's no such adage for tequila. Probably because it effects each person in a different way. It makes me horny, it makes you sleepy, and it makes Natalie argumentative."

I would have selected a different word. Mean or cruel would have been much more appropriate.

"But was she right?"

Jennifer had sighed loud enough to wake the dead. "What good would it do if I said yes? You'd just find a way to let me down easy."

"I haven't had my final fling yet. There's still time for me to turn you into a cliché."

Another joke. And a bad one at that. Apparently, tequila also makes me insensitive.

"One night with you wouldn't be enough for me, Syd. It would just be the beginning."

The seriousness of Jennifer's response—and the apparent

sincerity behind it—had taken my breath away. "What am I going to do without you?" I had wanted to put my arms around her and beg her to tell me everything was going to be okay, but with drowsiness setting in, my limbs had felt so heavy I hadn't been able to force them to move. "Tell me this isn't the end of us."

"There'll never be an end. Not for us. Wherever I am, I'll always be there for you. But you have Jack now. You don't need me anymore."

"I'll always need you."

"But *he's* the one you said you wanted. *He's* the one you said you've been looking for. He's also the absolute worst basketball player in the world, but if you can live with that, so can I."

Jennifer had stayed with me until I had fallen asleep. She'd returned the next morning to nurse me through the ensuing hangover—and to see me through the biggest day of my life. The next week, she had caught a plane to Darfur and I'd thought I'd lost her forever.

On the video, Natalie won the catfight for my wedding bouquet, coming out of the pile with the battered and bruised flowers. "So," she said, turning to Jennifer, "are we moving to Canada or Massachusetts?"

The answer had been neither. They'd broken up a few months later, when Jennifer had decided she could make better use of her medical skills in drought-stricken Africa than the Windy City. For Jennifer, it had been the start of a new kind of love affair—the one between her and the Dark Continent. Her stays there had grown longer and longer, her visits to the U.S. shorter and shorter until Natalie had decided she was over it.

"I want a girlfriend who's going to fuck me in person, not over the phone," she had said. "When you're here, your mind's there. And when you're there, I never hear from you. I'm tired of watching the news praying I won't see your name appear in the scroll at the bottom of the screen. 'Crusading American doctor Jennifer Rekowski murdered in East Africa.'"

I ejected the tape and returned it to its place on the shelf.

"What are you doing?" Jack asked.

I turned to face him. "Remembering."

Chapter Fourteen

W e have to talk," I said.
"I agree, but can we talk over lunch? I'm starving."

"What I have to say isn't for public consumption. It shouldn't be unexpected, but that doesn't mean it won't come as a bit of a shock."

"That sounds ominous. What is it?"

I could see him steeling himself as if he were one of his patients preparing himself to receive bad news.

"There's no easy way to say it so I'll just say it." I took a deep breath and spoke the words no wife ever expects to say. "I want a divorce."

Jack sat down hard. He took a moment to gather himself. When he was able to speak, he was a great deal more composed than I would have been if the shoe were on the other foot. "Three questions immediately come to mind: why, how long have you felt this way, and is there someone else?"

I wanted to break it to him gently, if such a thing existed.

"You are everything I'm supposed to want." I needed to explain the situation to him as well as myself. "I feel more comfortable with you than any man I've ever met. Even when

I realized that my heart was somewhere else, I thought I could make it work, but I can't. Jack, I'm—"

"Whatever you're about to say, don't. I love you, Syd," he said, trying to reassure me—and himself. "We can work it out."

"It's too late for that."

"What about this afternoon? That didn't feel like good-bye. Not to me."

"It did to me." To me, it had felt like the final nail in the coffin.

"There *is* someone else, isn't there?" He was trying to cast the blame elsewhere instead of placing it where it belonged: on me.

"It doesn't matter."

"It matters to me," he said sharply. "It would help me understand why you keep pushing me away when all I want to do is help you. Were you—*Are* you having an affair?" His voice was tiny. Choked. As if the emotions he was fighting back were too much for him.

"No," I replied. "One night is not an affair."

It took him a moment to fully grasp what I'd just said.

"One—So you have—With who?" he sputtered. "And don't try to tell me that it doesn't matter. I can't think of anything that matters more."

"I never thought anything would happen between us. I thought we had missed our chance. But when I saw her—"

"*Her?*" he asked, jumping on the slip. "You cheated on me with a *woman*? Most men wouldn't call that cheating. Unfortunately for you, I'm not most men. Who was she? That Marcy person? That would explain why she cleared out of here so fast, but please don't tell me you were willing to throw away our marriage for a roll in the hay with someone who drives a souped-up tricycle for a living."

"This isn't about her," I said. "It has nothing to do with her. She was a friend when I needed one, nothing more."

"If you didn't sleep with her, if she's simply an innocent bystander and doesn't have anything to do with us, then tell me who does. Or do I even have to guess? It's Jennifer, isn't it?"

I didn't answer him. My silence was enough.

"Of course it is," he said. "Who else would it be? She's the only person in this world you seem to give a damn about. I knew you were close, but not *that* close. You swore to me that nothing had ever happened between you two."

During the middle of our first date, he had asked me if Jennifer and I were an item. I had told him that Jennifer was gay and I wasn't, but it wasn't a problem for us because she and I were just friends. He had made me attest to the just friends bit on our third date, when we had started moving from casual to serious.

"At that point, nothing had."

"So when did that change?" A look of recognition crossed his face. "Never mind. I already know. It was last week. The night she got back from her latest mercy mission. I offered to sleep at the hospital so you two could stay up all night and play catch-up. You played catch-up all right. You used the opportunity to take advantage of my faith in you. In us. So how was it?" he asked bitterly.

"That really isn't your concern."

"As long as you're married to me, it's my concern. I haven't signed my name on the dotted line yet so you're still my wife. Tell me how it was. What did she do for you that I couldn't?"

I didn't have to fake it with her the way I did with him. Was that what he wanted to hear? Had I expected him to be happy for me? To wish me well? On some level, I suppose

I had. Otherwise, his vehemence wouldn't have stunned me nearly as much as it did.

"Jack, please don't make this hard for me," I said.

He let out a snort of disgust. "Why should I make it easy?"

He had a point. I had done to him what I wouldn't do to Marcy. I had led him on.

"It's over. Just let me go."

"If it's freedom you want, you can have it. You've always had it. But I deserve an explanation. What am I supposed to tell everyone?"

"The truth."

"I don't know what that is," he said with a rueful laugh. "Does Jennifer know about this? Did she put you up to it?"

"No one puts me up to anything. You know that. If it makes you feel any better, the last time I saw her, she told me to forget I ever met her. For a while, I did. Quite literally, in fact. But that's behind me now."

"What's in front of you?"

"The chance to finally be myself. And I'm going to take it."

"No matter who you hurt?"

The pointed question had an unexpected sting.

"Would you rather I stay with you and pretend or leave and be happy?" I asked.

"You can be happy with me," he insisted.

"How am I supposed to do that when you can't give me what I want?"

"I can look the other way if I have to."

"I could never ask you to do that."

"You're not asking me. I'm offering."

"I can't commit fifty percent of me to you and fifty percent

n Medias Res*

to someone else. It's all or nothing. Anything less than that wouldn't be fair to either of us."

"Who are you to decide what's fair and what isn't?"

"Who are you to decide what's not? You said you wanted a marriage based on honesty. What you're proposing isn't what I'd call honest."

"It could be. If we were adults about it."

"I don't want an open marriage, Jack."

"It sounds like you don't want a closed one, either."

"I do," I said, "but not with you."

I took off my rings and placed them in his hand.

"Syd, don't do this. If I don't understand, how can you expect your parents to? Or anyone else, for that matter?"

"You don't have to understand me. Just respect me and the effort I put into making this decision."

He squeezed my discarded rings in his palm, undoubtedly thinking back to the day he'd slipped them on my finger as we promised to love each other until death do us part. "There's nothing I can say to convince you to change your mind?"

I slowly shook my head.

"Then I want you to give Jennifer a message for me."

It was my turn to steel myself for what he was about to say.

"You tell her that if she hurts you, she'll have to answer to me."

We held each other and cried the way we had never allowed ourselves to when we were together. In time, I thought we could be friends, provided we worked hard enough at it and wanted it badly enough. With the pain I had inflicted still too fresh in his mind, the last thing Jack wanted or needed was to be around me. Fine by me. I had a plane to catch—and history to rewrite.

Chapter Fifteen

I was alone when my taxi showed up. Alone and wondering if I would always be that way.

The cabbie stuck his head out the driver's side window. "Somebody here call for a pick-up?"

"Yeah, I did."

I pushed myself off the steps and helped him load up.

"Which airline?" he asked, making notations on the clipboard that hung from the glove compartment.

"United."

I had booked the first flight available to Chicago. If I knew where Jennifer was, I would have joined her there, even though the last time I saw her, she'd said that wasn't what she wanted.

"I won't be the lie you tell," she had written—after helping me uncover the truth.

I would try to track her down soon enough. But first things first. I needed to go home. I needed to see my family.

I called my brother while I was standing in line at the sidewalk check-in. The small airport was unexpectedly busy. Almost as if a hurricane were bearing down on the island and all the tourists had been ordered to evacuate.

"This is Pat."

I could hear testosterone-filled voices in the background. The Bears were preparing for Sunday's playoff game with the Cowboys. Patrick was probably working on the backup running back's gimpy left ankle. With Chicago's ball-control offense, the team would need as many people to carry the load as possible.

"I'm calling a meeting of Team Paulsen and I need to know if you're free tonight."

"What time will you be getting in?"

"My flight lands at five, which means I'll have to fight my way through airport *and* drive-time traffic."

"Then why don't we meet at my place? It's closer."

Patrick's house was a stone's throw from the airport. My parents' house was way out in the 'burbs.

"Are you sure Kristin won't mind?"

"I'll check with her, but I don't see why she would. You're family, not company so we won't have to run around picking up the kids' toys in order to make the place presentable for you. Is there anything else you need me to do?"

"I'm about to check in so I don't have time to make a ton of phone calls. Can you call Mom and Dad and get them on board? Tell them we'll meet them at your house at seven. I'll take over from there."

"I can do that. Do I get a hint about the topic of tonight's meeting?"

"Sorry, no home field advantage."

"Oh, well. Can't blame a guy for trying. See ya tonight, sis."

The flight to Miami was short and sweet. A brief layover at Miami International gave me just enough time to have a watered-down drink and overpriced sandwich in one of the airport restaurants. I spent the flight to Chicago practicing what I was going to say. By the time I landed, I still didn't have it down pat. All I needed was an opening. Once I got started, I would be fine. But I couldn't figure out a way to set the table. Should I begin with a joke or should I simply dive right in?

After enduring the interminable wait for my luggage at O'Hare, I spent a good fifteen minutes trying to find my car in the long-term parking lot. I had lost my ticket stub before my flight to Key West. At the time, remembering the number of my parking spot hadn't been very high on my list of priorities. I found my car by pressing the panic button on my keychain until I got close enough to my car to set off the alarm.

I tossed my bags in the trunk and drove to Patrick and Kristin's subdivision. I parked my two-year-old BMW next to Dad's ten-year-old Ford Taurus, the deadly dull but dependable vehicle he had steadfastly refused to part with despite my many offers of a complimentary upgrade.

"I don't care how a car looks as long as it gets me where I'm going," he had said time and time again. "It's what's under the hood that counts. The rest is just pretty packaging."

It's what's inside that counts. I hoped he would continue to feel that way even after I shared the feelings that were churning inside me.

Patrick opened the front door before I could ring the bell. "Anxious much?" I asked as he closed the door behind me. He shadowed me as I hung my hat and coat in the hall closet.

"Let's see. The last time you called a family meeting, it was to tell us you were quitting your six-figure job for one with an annual salary of, um, zero. Now Mom thinks you're either dying or having a baby. So, yeah, I'm a little anxious to hear what's going on with you. The floor's yours."

He tossed me the ancient Spalding football that had been present at every family meeting since I was nine years old. The person who held the ball during the meeting was the only person allowed to speak. Each Paulsen respected the power of the football. Its privileges had been abused only once—when Patrick had attempted to convince Mom and Dad that his first vehicle should be a Harley instead of a Taurus. He had filibustered for hours on gas mileage comparisons, safety concerns, and "the coolness factor." When all was said and done, he ended up with a wicked case of laryngitis—and a brand-new Taurus.

I tucked the football in my arm like I was a running back looking for daylight.

My audience consisted of only four people, but my heart pounded as if I were about to give a speech to four hundred. My parents, my brother, and my sister-in-law were looking at me with such trepidation that I knew I had to get to the point and fast.

"Before I begin, let me ease your minds by saying this isn't a matter of life and death."

"Oh, thank God," my mother said, momentarily forgetting the ground rules. She covered her mouth apologetically and waved at me to go on.

"You've undoubtedly noticed that Jack isn't with me. He knows we're here and he knows what I intend to discuss with you. I have his support and I hope I'll have yours."

My mouth went dry and I struggled to swallow.

"This isn't a matter of life and death, but it is a matter of the heart. My heart hasn't been in my marriage for a while." I took another calming breath. "Before I left Key West, I asked Jack for a divorce and he agreed to give me one."

My mother reached for the box of tissues someone had placed on the coffee table before my arrival.

"Even though I have feelings for someone else," I continued, "I didn't leave Jack for someone else. I left him for me. I left him because I was finally able to admit I'm not what he needs and he isn't what I want."

I looked at my dad. I wanted him, more than anyone else, to hear what I had to say. He had been my biggest fan when I was growing up but also, in a way, my biggest detractor. By adhering to his edicts, I had excised a vital part of myself. A part that, like a phantom limb, I had continued to feel if not see. A part that had grown back.

With his gruff exterior and Far Right political stance, Dad was like Archie Bunker without the comedic flush. Mom was a less ditzy Edith.

I had set impossible goals for myself. Dad had set impossible standards. Standards I could no longer meet. He was the one I had always tried to please. The one I had always wanted to make proud. I still wanted to do that, but it was time for me to live by another set of rules. Rules I had stubbornly insisted did not apply to me.

"I want Jennifer." I almost laughed at how ridiculously good it felt to say that out loud.

Three words. Three simple words. Why had it taken me so long to utter them?

"I have done everything you've ever asked me to do. Now I'm asking you to return the favor: accept me as I am, not who you wish me to be."

I placed the football on the table, opening the floor for comments. The explosion I had expected didn't come. Mom, Dad, Patrick, and Kristin looked at each other, but no one moved. Finally, after what felt like an eternity, Dad reached out and picked up the ball.

"Are you sure this is what you want to do?"

Even though he had asked me a question, he didn't give me the ball back so I could answer it. I nodded yes.

"You've been unhappy for years and I didn't know what to do to fix it. It's a father's job, you know. To fix things. But I couldn't fix you." His voice shook as he examined the faded lettering on the ball. "I want you to be happy. If Jennifer makes you happy, I'm all for it."

He came over to me and gave me a bear hug. "I love you, Sydney," he whispered in my ear. "Be happy."

I knew my father loved me, but I couldn't remember the last time I had heard him say it.

"I'm going to try," I said, trying not to get choked up.

Mom was crying too much to say more than a few words. When she held me, I couldn't fathom how her tiny little body could possess such strength. She looked at me, her eyes watery but filled with love. "What he said," she croaked.

I—and everyone else—assumed Patrick would speak next. When he didn't, Kristin picked up the slack. "Today's the first day of the rest of your life," she said. "How does it feel?"

"I feel like I've been holding my breath for thirty-one years and I'm finally able to breathe."

She hugged me again. "I'm so happy for you, Syd. Congratulations." She placed the ball on the table and sat back down. She looked at Patrick. When he remained motionless, she dug an elbow into his ribs.

Patrick reached for the football. His bushy eyebrows were knitted into an unmistakable frown. "I don't mean to piss in your cornflakes, but I'm not happy with you right now." Kristin put a placating hand on his arm but he shook it off. "No, I've got to say this." He turned back to me. I had expected resistance from Mom and Dad but not from him. "I'm your brother and I'll love you no matter what. I've had your back since day one and I always will. Don't you know that?"

"I—"

Patrick waved the Spalding over his head like he was doing a touchdown dance. "Respect the football," he reminded me.

I let him have the floor.

"Let me be the first to say I saw this coming. I knew it was a mistake for you to marry Jack, but I knew better than to try to talk you out of it. Once you make up your mind about something, no one and nothing can force you to change it. No one except you."

He pointed the ball at me to emphasize his point.

"I thought Jennifer could talk some sense into you. When you and Jack were dating, I asked her if she thought you were…" He waved the ball in the air to indicate I should complete his sentence with the word of my choosing. "She said it didn't matter what she thought. Your opinion of yourself was the only one that counted. You have the biggest balls of anyone I know. I'm disappointed it took you this long to look yourself in the mirror and like what you see."

So was I.

"But—and this is the important part, so please pay attention." He stood in front of me and put a hand on my shoulder. "If you love Jennifer as much as you say you do, what are you doing here?" He pressed the football into my midsection like a quarterback handing off to a runner. "Go get her."

Chapter Sixteen

I had a plane to catch. Unlike the day before, I didn't have a ticket in my hand to tell me my destination. I would need Marcus's help for that.

The apartment he and Jennifer shared was located in Lakeview, the neighborhood nicknamed Boystown for its many venues that catered mainly to gay men. After driving to the North Side in near-record time, I rang the bell and waited for Marcus to answer.

"You lied to me," I said before he could even say hello. "I checked with every relief agency Jennifer has ever worked for and each of them told me the same thing: she isn't in Darfur."

"It's good to see you, too, Syd. How are you?"

I knew I was being rude, but I didn't have time for pleasantries. "Where is she, Marcus?"

"I'm not supposed to tell you."

"Did she tell you about us?"

"That's why I'm not supposed to tell you."

"Is that why you gave me the runaround yesterday? When you led me to believe she was in the desert when you knew she wasn't?"

"What was I supposed to do, pat you on the back? You broke her heart, Syd."

"I know. That means I'm the only one who can mend it. Tell me where she is, Marcus. Please."

"So you can do what? Choose Jack over her for the third time? No can do." He sat in front of the bank of computers he used to run his at-home I.T. company. "I heard he took some time off so you two could have a second honeymoon. Is that true?"

I grabbed the back of Marcus's desk chair and spun him around to face me. "No, the honeymoon's over. Permanently."

"No shit?" he asked skeptically.

"No shit. Giving up on her was the biggest mistake I've ever made in my life," I said, trying to help him along. "Please help me fix it."

"I promised her I wouldn't tell you."

"Please."

"Do you have any idea what you're asking me to do? Do you know what you'd be getting into?"

"Yes, on both counts. Marcus, I love her. Please."

He sighed deeply. "Okay," he said at last. "She's in Honduras. Blake's clinic is finally beginning to make some inroads in both the local and indigenous communities. Jen offered to help him out for a while. But you didn't hear that from me."

"Hear what?" I teased him.

Twenty minutes and six hundred dollars later, I was booked on a six a.m. flight on American Airlines to Tegucigalpa via Miami. From there, I would take a bumpy three-hour bus ride to Puerto Lempira. Jennifer was in Mocoron, a tiny town forty miles to the south.

I was too wound up to sleep, despite the ten hours of travel time that loomed in front of me. Waiting for the clock to tick down to the beginning of the next leg of my journey, I thought back to the night my voyage of self-discovery had begun.

Chapter Seventeen

Jennifer's flight landed at three p.m. Her parents, Ed and Maureen, picked her up at the airport. I wanted to do it—I'd done everything else, from planning the party to picking the restaurant to selecting the items on the menu—but I thought the three of them could use some quiet time together before the rest of us began vying for Jennifer's attention. She hadn't been home in nearly six months. Though we all had missed her, her parents had missed her more.

They would spend three hours getting reacquainted, then join the rest of us at Jennifer's favorite Greek restaurant at six.

I got to Athena's an hour early so I could check out the setup and greet the early arrivals. Sitting in the empty banquet room, I enjoyed the quiet before the storm. The servers hustled in and out, bringing in trays of cold cuts and turning on the burners for the warm dishes. They had their job to do and I had mine. So, for the most part, we left each other alone.

My parents were first on the scene. They showed up half an hour before the scheduled start. "Need any help?" Mom asked, rolling up her sleeves. I was taping up a Welcome Home sign and she wanted to pitch in.

"No, I think the staff has everything under control." I secured the last piece of tape and stepped down off the chair

I had been using as a makeshift ladder. Dad gave me a quick hug, then handed me a brightly wrapped box. "Is this for Jen?" I asked, looking for the gift card. "What did you buy her?"

"I stopped by the Army surplus store and picked up some MREs."

I held the box away from me as if it might blow. "Meals, Ready-to-Eat? Ew."

Created for military personnel to take with them into the field, MREs were vacuum-sealed rations that could be eaten right out of the package. The small flexible containers were filled with an appetizer, an entrée, condiments, and a couple of desserts. Armed with a flameless heater and a spoon, you could "enjoy" anything from chicken tetrazzini to beef enchiladas to turkey and dressing. Dad swore by them. When Mom went on her annual pilgrimage to Atlantic City with her bridge club each June, the whole week she was gone, Dad eschewed the casseroles she had frozen in advance. Instead, he wolfed down MREs like they were going out of style.

Leave it to Dad to be both thoughtful and practical. Under his gruff exterior beat a heart of gold—even if you had to dig deep to find it. I wished Jack could be more like him. Vain and occasionally arrogant, Jack had a tendency to put himself first—except when it came to me. He treated me as if I were fine china, the kind that would break if you handled it too roughly. Some women might consider that behavior sweet. I found it annoying. Tough as nails, I was far from fragile.

"Don't be that way," Dad said, wagging his finger at me like he was lecturing me about breaking curfew. "They taste a lot better now than they did when I was in the service."

"Even if they didn't, they've got to be better than what she's eating over there," Mom said. She spoke out of the corner of her mouth, trying not to be overheard even though we were the only guests present. "Bread, beans, and water? They get more than that on *Survivor*."

"But on *Survivor*, the backstabbing is figurative, not literal," I said. "No one tries to put a bullet in your head when you leave the camp to collect firewood. The worst they can do is vote you off. I think Jennifer would prefer that any day."

"If that's true, then why doesn't she come home?"

I asked myself that question all the time. I admired her selflessness, but I couldn't emulate her example. I wanted her home. I wanted her safe. I wanted her with me, not halfway around the world.

"She's home now," I said. "That's all that matters."

Jack burst through the door as if his hair were on fire. He apologized to the waitress he had nearly bowled over and began to beg for my forgiveness as well. I tapped my watch, indicating the time.

"I know. I know," he said, trying to placate me. "I got stuck in pediatrics."

"Nothing bad, I hope," Mom said. She shook her head empathetically. "There's nothing worse than a sick child."

"This one's fine," Jack said. "An eight-year-old who swallowed his sister's class ring because she wouldn't let him hang out with her and her friends. She wouldn't let me leave until he passed it and he held on to it as long as he could just to spite her. He forgot about all that once the third dose of laxatives kicked in."

"Did everything come out okay?" Dad asked.

Mom smacked him on the arm. "Sidney, that's disgusting. Don't make jokes like that so close to the food."

"Yeah, Dad," I chimed in. "If you contaminate the souvlaki, we'll be forced to break open these MREs."

He patted his stomach. "They'll fill you up a lot faster than that rabbit food you're going to be feeding us."

I tucked the box under the buffet table for safekeeping. If anyone else brought a present, the servers and I would have some rearranging to do in order to create a display area for gifts. There might be room on the dessert table, but not much. I had to save ample space for the baklava or there would be hell to pay. Jennifer didn't have much of a sweet tooth, but her friends sure did. They had me outnumbered.

Everyone started to stream in around six fifteen. Jennifer's friends from college, work, and around town. The lesbian rec league softball team she used to play for—the Dyke Daddies—showed up en masse.

Natalie showed up, too—with her new girlfriend in tow. Jennifer and Natalie's split had not been a smooth one. I wondered if their reunion would be just as tumultuous. Lindsay's presence wouldn't help matters much.

I hadn't been around her enough to form an opinion of her. I had met her once when Dad and I ran into her and Natalie at a Bulls game. (Dad had season tickets. Mom didn't like any sports and Patrick preferred football to basketball, so I was Dad's usual date.)

Natalie had introduced us at halftime. She had spent the rest of the game trying to arrange a double date with me and Jack. When she and Jennifer were together and Jack and I were dating, the four of us got together for dinner once a week. Natalie was anxious to revive the tradition.

"Just because I broke up with Jennifer doesn't mean I broke up with you, does it?" she had asked. "*Our* relationship doesn't have to end."

Actually, yes, it did. I was Jennifer's best friend. As such, it was against the rules for me to be friends with her ex if she wasn't on good terms with her. Considering my confrontation with Natalie the night before my wedding, I wasn't on good terms with her either.

"Great party," Lindsay said on her way back from the open bar, a drink in each hand.

"Thanks," I replied. Though Lindsay seemed okay, I was

prepared to dislike her out of loyalty to Jen. I watched her cross the room. She handed Natalie an apple martini and kept a White Russian for herself.

Jennifer and her parents showed up around six thirty. She looked good. Great, in fact. Her blond hair had been bleached almost platinum by the sun. Though it had once fallen past her shoulders, it was now so short she could comb it with her fingers. Out of convenience, no doubt. No time to wash and blow dry when you're dodging armed men on horseback.

She had lost at least fifteen pounds since the last time I'd seen her, but the weight loss looked good on her. She looked vibrant, not anorexic. She practically hummed with energy.

Swarmed right away, it took her nearly an hour to free herself to say hello to me. "Nice party," she said, munching on a carrot stick. "Where's the real food?"

"You sound like Dad," I said, watching him load up his saucer-sized plate with miniature gyros. "Don't worry. Back at my apartment, I've got a steak with your name on it."

She grinned, her blue eyes sparkling in her deeply tanned face. "I think I love you."

She pulled me into her arms and my heart lurched in my chest. It had been so long since I had seen her that I didn't want to let go. "You're going to be home for a while, right?" I asked, holding on to her whittled waist.

"At least three months—if you can stand having me around that long."

"I think I can manage."

Holding me at arm's length, she looked me up and down. "You look happy," she said.

"That's because I'm looking at you." I smiled and touched her cheek. The gesture must have been too personal—too intimate—for her liking. She stiffened at the contact, as if she were enduring it for my benefit. I was so excited to see her that

I had failed to take into account how much it must have hurt for her to see me. Abashed, I drew my hand away.

"What's this I hear about you quitting your job?" she asked.

"That's a long story. This isn't the time or the place. I'll tell you later."

"Syd."

"It's not a cop-out. I promise I'll tell you later."

"You'd better." She changed the subject to something else I didn't want to talk about. "How are you and Jack?"

"We're fine," I answered a little too quickly.

She dropped her eyes to my stomach. "No news to report?"

"No," I said firmly. I relented a bit, dulling the edge that had crept into my voice. "Jack wants kids and his mother wants grandkids, but I'm not so sure. In many ways, I'm still a kid myself. The female version of Peter Pan."

"When do you plan on growing up?"

"I'm putting that off as long as I can."

"Wise move. Innocence is precious. You don't want to lose it." She sounded as if she had lost hers a long time ago.

"I don't want to lose you, either. When are you going to make me stop worrying about you?" I had promised I wouldn't ask her that question, but I couldn't help myself.

"You'd worry about me even if I were here and you know it."

She had me dead to rights. Worrying about her was a habit of mine. One I didn't intend to break.

"Someone's got to do it," I said. "Why not me?"

Her eyes found Jack and returned to me. "Because you have someone else to worry about now."

"But what if I—"

"Jen, hi." Natalie wandered over to say hello and to introduce Jennifer to Lindsay. "Sorry to interrupt, Syd."

"It's okay," I said. "I was just leaving." Not wanting to make the situation more awkward than it already was, I turned to go. Jennifer held me in place with a look. "Or not."

"Don't you dare leave me alone with her," Jennifer's eyes pleaded. So I didn't.

"Don't I get a hug?" Natalie asked.

"Of course," Jennifer replied, doling out a halfhearted squeeze.

"It's good to see you again."

"You, too."

Natalie drew Lindsay into the conversation, leaving me as the only one without a date to the dance. "Jen, this is Lindsay. Lindsay, Jen."

"I've heard a lot about you," Lindsay said. "Now I can finally put a face to the name. It's nice to meet you." She extended her hand.

"You, too," Jennifer replied, pumping Lindsay's hand once and letting go. "Do you know Sydney?"

"Yes, we've met," Lindsay said with a nod in my direction. "Hiya, Syd."

"Hey."

"How long have you been seeing each other?" Jennifer asked.

"We've been dating for a couple of months," Natalie said, wrapping her arm around Lindsay's waist. "Things are going really well."

"So well, in fact, that we've decided to move in together," Lindsay added.

Jennifer looked to Natalie for confirmation. Natalie nodded that it was true. Cohabitating was a step Natalie had been unable to get Jennifer to take, even though they had been an item for nearly six years before they had broken up. Jennifer had always said she was too comfortable living with Marcus to move out. I thought she was hedging her bets if, for some reason, the relationship with Natalie didn't work out.

"I'm happy for you," Jennifer said. "Really. Good luck."

"Thanks. That means a lot," Natalie said. She took a sip of her drink before asking the question that was on all our minds. "Are you seeing anyone?"

Jennifer shook her head. "I was for a while but it's over. Work got in the way."

"That's becoming a common theme for you. Perhaps you'll find a solution for it one day," Natalie said. She squeezed Jennifer's elbow, even though a hug was called for. "Take care of yourself, okay?"

"You, too." Jennifer watched them walk away. "That was harder than I thought," she said once they were out of earshot. When she turned back to me, her eyes had lost some of their previous luster.

"Were you hoping for a reconciliation?" I asked.

"No, but I do regret the way our relationship ended. I could have handled the situation better than I did. Every time I see her, I feel like an ass. But she's moved on and so have I."

"Then everything worked out for the best." I hugged her again. I had to keep touching her to convince myself she was real and not a mirage. "I missed you like crazy."

"Same here." So she said. She seemed less excited to see me than I was to see her. But could I blame her? She indicated her former teammates. "The girls are going to take me out for a drink once this is over. I'll try to make it fast. I'll see you around ten, no later than eleven. Is that good?"

I had rented the banquet room from six to eight. It would take me at least half an hour to see everyone off and another half to get home. If Jennifer made her usual rounds—from Stargaze to T's to Joie De Vine with a pit stop for Hawaiian burgers at Tomboy or tapas at Arco De Cuchilleros on the way—that would be more than enough time.

"That's perfect. See you then."

She headed off to re-join her friends. I left to find Jack. A glass of white wine in his hand, he was grazing at the buffet table.

The menu was informal. Heavy on finger foods and hors d'oeuvres, the strategically placed food stations allowed guests to munch and mingle at the same time. Regaling all who would listen with stories of her wild adventures, Jennifer wouldn't have time to eat. No problem. I had planned for that, too. When the gathering ended, I would take her back to my apartment and fire up the indoor grill. She could eat—and we could talk—in peace. Provided, of course, I found a way to get rid of Jack. I didn't want him and Jennifer to spend the rest of the evening sniping at each other the way they usually did. I had to keep them apart somehow or all my planning would have been for naught.

Jack attacked the tray of bacon-wrapped dates, popping one after another into his mouth. "Where are the T-bones you promised me?"

"I think I promised you something other than steak," I replied, rubbing his shoulders.

"You haven't spoiled me like this in months." He groaned when my fingers found an especially tight spot. "Jennifer should come home more often."

The tension I had just released from his shoulders settled into mine. I was having an increasingly difficult time keeping my two lives separate: the one I had with Jack and the one I dreamed about having with Jennifer. I wanted to be with her, but had she moved on from me as she had with Natalie? There was only one way to find out, but I was too chicken to take the first step. Not to sound conceited, but I could have any man I wanted. What would I do, though, if the woman I wanted didn't want me?

"You know how much Jen loves red meat. The beef is for her, not you. She probably hasn't had any since she left."

Jack arched his eyebrows mischievously. "Knowing Jennifer, I doubt that."

"Don't start," I said. I reached for an olive stuffed with feta cheese. I washed down the salty confection with a shot of ouzo. "Do I need to keep you two separated tonight?"

"Probably," he said. Taking a sip of his wine, he watched Jennifer hold court on the other side of the room. Her former life as an ER doc had been exciting enough, but her new life made the old one seem tame. Jack looked envious.

Marcus and his boyfriend Trevor came over to say hello. "If you're giving out free massages, I'll take one," Marcus said.

"Sorry. First come, first served. Jack got the last one." I greeted Trevor, then turned back to Marcus. "Are you going to be able to adjust to having a roommate again?"

With Jennifer gone, he and Trevor had had the apartment to themselves.

"I don't think she's going to be around much," Marcus said. "She's got some catching up to do."

I thought he had meant work until I saw a gorgeous brunette slip Jennifer her phone number.

"Looks like you missed your chance," Marcus whispered in my ear. "Again."

Marcus and Trevor left to mingle with the other guests and I turned around to find Jack hoarding the *dolmathes*—grape leaves stuffed with ground beef, rice, and mint.

"Since you and Jennifer are going to be up half the night

talking and I've got an early shift tomorrow, why don't I crash at the hospital?" he asked, licking his fingers. "That way, I can get some sleep and you can play catch-up all you want."

The idea thrilled me in a primal way, but I tried to temper my excitement. Jack was so sensitive where Jennifer was concerned that I didn't want him to think that I was trying to get rid of him. Even though I was. "Are you sure?"

He picked up a potato dumpling. "If I hear one more story about Africa, I'll go postal. You can give me the CliffsNotes version of events tomorrow night."

The party began to break up around eight fifteen, just in time for the evening rush.

Jennifer said a few words before everyone headed out the door. "In case I didn't thank each of you individually, let me thank you collectively for coming tonight. You didn't have to and I appreciate it. An even bigger thank you to Sydney for doing this for me in the first place. It means a lot to me. Even more than you know. Thanks, Syd."

Her voice broke a little at the end and we all went "Awww," but one of her teammates put the kibosh on the unexpected show of emotion. "You're welcome, now let's go get laid!" she catcalled.

"I'll drink to that," Jennifer said. She polished off her beer and swept out the door. Everyone else soon followed.

Jack walked me to my car. He stood guard as I placed the floral centerpiece from the dessert table in my passenger's seat and secured it with the seat belt. When I climbed into the driver's seat and switched on the ignition, the powerful engine roared to life. Jack rapped his knuckles on the windshield. I decreased the volume on the Rolling Stones' *Greatest Hits* CD blaring out of the speakers and lowered the driver's side window.

"Are you going to be all right?" he asked.

"Sure. Why wouldn't I be?"

He searched his pockets for his keys. "I don't want you to hold it against me for skipping out on your hen party." He tossed the lint and deli receipt he unearthed and resumed his search.

I leaned out the window, reached into the inside pocket of his jacket—his usual hiding place—and retrieved his keys. "It's okay," I said, dangling the key ring in front of him. "No cocks allowed."

"Just the way Jennifer likes it." He kissed the back of my hand like a courtly lover. "I'm glad I know you feel differently. Otherwise, I might be a little nervous about you spending the night with her."

"It was your idea, remember?"

"I hope I don't live to regret it."

"So do I."

Cranking up the volume on "Gimme Shelter," I sped toward home. I stowed my car in the parking garage and walked the two blocks to my apartment building. I took the stairs instead of the elevator so I could burn off some energy. I needed to pull myself back from the ledge I found myself peeking over. I felt on the verge of something. Something major. Something foolish. Something that could change my life forever.

I was out of breath when I reached my floor but no closer to being in control. I unlocked the door and went inside. "It's okay," I told myself as I stood in the dark. "You're not going to do this and she's not going to let you. It's okay."

Yeah, I didn't believe it, either. I was far from okay. I wanted Jennifer so much it hurt, but I feared she wouldn't be receptive to anything I might propose. If she spent six months at a time in a Sudanese desert to get away from me, why would she let me get close? Out of self-preservation, she would probably continue to keep me at a distance. I knew all about that. I was doing the same thing to Jack. Every time he tried to break through my defenses, I fortified them even more. It wasn't fair to him and it wasn't fair to me, but I didn't have time to face it because I was too busy trying to salvage what was left of my career. The stress was overwhelming and I didn't know how much more I could take.

I placed the floral arrangement on the dining room table. In the bedroom, I ditched my party clothes for a T-shirt and a pair of boxers. Off went the heels, on went the thick cotton socks and Bugs Bunny slippers. I had been wearing a mask at the party. The more things I removed, the more I felt like myself. Whoever that was.

In the kitchen, I pulled out the grill and primed it with a couple of shots of nonstick cooking spray. I grabbed the bag of T-bones out of the refrigerator and tossed it on the counter to give the steaks time to come to room temperature before I dropped them onto the grill.

I wrapped a couple of potatoes in aluminum foil and placed them on a cookie sheet. The oversized Russets would need at least an hour to bake, so I preheated the oven and shoved the potatoes inside when the temperature indicator went ding.

Prep work done, I had time to relax for the first time in hours. I pulled out my favorite movie, *The Usual Suspects*, and put my feet up.

I soon lost track of time. When Jennifer rang the buzzer downstairs, it was almost ten thirty.

"Cute outfit," she said when I let her in.

"Didn't you know? It's what all the well-dressed women in Chicago are wearing these days."

"I'll take your word for it." She kissed me on the cheek as if she were greeting me for the first time that day. "Where's Jack?" she asked, looking around.

"He decided to make himself scarce tonight. It's just you and me."

"I see."

"Is that bad?" I wanted her to feel comfortable, not trapped.

"No, just unexpected."

"Are you hungry?"

"Famished."

I turned on the burners to heat the grill. "Did you have fun tonight?"

"Yeah, the party was great. Thanks again." I didn't have to offer her anything to drink. Making herself at home, she grabbed a bottle of water out of the refrigerator.

"I meant after the party." I lowered one of the two thick T-bone steaks onto the grill. "How many phone numbers did you end up with?"

The bottle of water paused on its way to her mouth. "A few."

"I can tell." I indicated the lipstick stain on the collar of her shirt. Cursing under her breath, she unbuttoned her shirt and headed to the bathroom to scrub the stain out. I waited for her to volunteer some information about who had put it there, but she held back. "The Resolve's under the sink," I called out.

"I remember." She rummaged around until she located the cleaner and a scrub brush.

"So tell me about this woman you were seeing," I said, giving the salad a quick toss before I carried the bowl to the dining room. "You didn't mention her in any of your e-mails. Why not?"

Whenever she was away, Jennifer e-mailed me every couple of weeks or so. Just a brief note to say hello and let me know she was still out there somewhere. I, on the other hand, wrote every day to remind her that I was here.

From my vantage point, I could see her reflection in the bathroom mirror. My hungry eyes roamed over her body until they got their fill. I watched the rainbow flag tattooed on her left arm wave back and forth as she vigorously scrubbed MAC lipstick out of her shirt collar.

"I didn't tell you about her because the relationship wasn't anything I needed to write home about," she said. "It was something she and I needed to do to maintain our sanity. I didn't love her. She didn't love me. At the time, it didn't matter. We had seen so much brutality that we needed to remind ourselves what tenderness felt like."

She hung her shirt on the back of the bathroom door and headed to the bedroom to borrow one of my T-shirts. She didn't have to ask because she already knew what the answer would be. What was mine was hers and vice versa.

"Who was she?" I flipped my steak and added Jennifer's to the grill. The meat sizzled as it came into contact with the hot cast iron.

"Her name was Viviane. Everyone called her Vivi. She was a trauma surgeon from Belgium. When patients came through triage, I stabilized them and she put them back together. I wouldn't mind working with her again someday—we made a great team—but I don't see that happening. Not unless I move to Antwerp. She went back there a few weeks after she arrived in camp. She underestimated how bad the conditions would be and the effect they would have on her psyche. Man's inhumanity to man and all that."

"If Vivi burned out after just a few weeks, how have you managed to stick it out for so long?"

"You know me. I like flying by the seat of my pants."

She came out of the bedroom wearing a University of Illinois T-shirt—the faded orange one I used to wear under my soccer jersey. Filled with a mixture of pride and possessiveness, I suddenly realized how guys felt when they saw their girlfriends parading around in their dress shirts after a night of deeply satisfying sex.

She's mine, I thought. *All mine.*

"Besides, I knew what I was signing up for," Jennifer said. "Vivi didn't. She came in expecting to work in a sterile, controlled environment like the one she had at home. Most days, the most technologically advanced pieces of equipment available were our left hands, our right hands, and some needle and thread. Vivi didn't like working without a net. I did. It helped me see what I was made of. Don't get me wrong. It's not all doom and gloom. Some days it's like an episode of *M*A*S*H*—a heavy dose of reality, followed by bursts of low humor. There are some good things that happen every now and then. The unexpected miracles that make your day."

Leaning against the counter, she launched into a story. One she hadn't told at the party. One I hadn't heard before.

"One day about four months ago, a little boy named Tshimanga was brought into camp. He was six years old, but he looked much younger. The relief workers called him Tiny Tim because he was so small. He had been hit with machine gun fire and his left leg was practically pulverized. I got his pressure stable, got him to surgery, and assisted in the operation. We didn't think we'd be able to save his leg and he had lost so much blood that amputation seemed like the best way to go, but his father told the surgical team that all Tim wanted to be when he grew up was a soccer player. He begged us not to take the leg. We managed to save it somehow.

"His left leg is going to be shorter than his right, so I don't know if he'll be able to play soccer when he grows up.

That may be an impossible dream. But what I do know is that when I left to come back here, he was starting to walk on his own. If you had seen him when he came in, you wouldn't have thought such a thing was possible. When he took his first step, his smile lit up the room. I knew then that I was in the right place. If not for stories like his, I would feel like I was fighting a losing battle. I'd be tempted to give up. But I don't because I know I'm doing the right thing."

"Don't you ever get scared, though?"

"Only every minute of every day. If I didn't, I'd know it was time for me to go into a new line of work. Whether I'm here or there, I have someone's life in my hands. That's not an easy thing to deal with. When you lose a patient, you feel responsible. Even if you know you've done everything you possibly could to save that person, the guilt overwhelms you. But I came home to take a break. Let's talk about something else for a while."

She uncorked a bottle of pinot noir, poured two glasses, and handed me one. Then she nearly made me choke on it.

"Let's talk about you," she said. "Why have you been out of a job for almost five months?"

"I wanted to tell you face-to-face, not via e-mail. But I thought you might hear it through the grapevine before I could."

"I've heard a version of the story," she said as we carried our plates to the table. "Now I want to hear yours."

I took the empty chair across from her and began to tell her about my trip from the penthouse to the outhouse.

"I don't have to tell you who Everett McDougald is. He's only one of the richest men in Chicago and my firm's—my *former* firm's largest client. He's had Beckmann, Warner, and Lowe on retainer for years. We—note how I still say *we*. *They* have helped him with everything from contract review to civil suits. You name it and we—*they* have done it for him. Five months ago, my phone rang in the middle of the night. It was four in the morning and my first thought was, 'Oh, God, who died?'"

"And you immediately thought of me."

"Naturally, but it wasn't about you. It was the senior partner calling me to tell me that Everett McDougald's son E. J. had been arrested after getting into a fight on the L and he was being charged with aggravated assault during the commission of a hate crime. The senior McDougald had a soft spot for me because of the work I'd done for him in the past and he insisted I be part of the defense team. When Howard Beckmann called me, he didn't just make me part of the team. He offered to make me first chair, which was a major vote of confidence. I started salivating right away and said yes without hearing any of the details. I didn't need to hear the details. All I knew was that with the McDougald name involved, it would be the kind of case that, if I won it, would put my name on the door."

"Corner office, here you come."

"So I thought. The call came on the weekend before my birthday, so I went back to bed thinking 'Happy birthday to me.'

"The arrest was all over the news the next day. That's when the details began to come out. E. J. and several of his fraternity brothers went bar hopping on Friday night. All of them got too hammered to drive so they decided to take the L home. By home, I don't mean the McDougald estate. If they had gone there, there wouldn't be a story. One of the members of the group has an apartment in the city so they decided to go there to keep the party going a while longer."

I took a quick sip of wine as the story got harder to tell.

"Jason Cooper, the victim in the case, boarded the train

at the Halsted stop. He didn't know E. J. from the man in the moon, but he thought he was cute so he smiled at him. E. J. took offense and started verbally abusing Jason on the train. E. J.'s a big guy—six-four, two hundred twenty pounds. Jason is half a foot shorter and fifty pounds lighter. He tried to defuse the situation, but E. J.'s friends—filled with a potent combination of testosterone and alcohol—inflamed it even more."

"The proverbial Greek chorus?" Jennifer asked.

"Exactly. When Jason got off the train at the next stop to try to prevent a confrontation, E. J. followed him. E. J. beat him up and slashed him in the face with a straight razor. He fled the scene thinking there were no witnesses, but a security camera caught the entire incident.

"When I met with the McDougalds on Sunday to hear E. J.'s side and plan my defense, E. J. confirmed that what the press had reported was accurate. He displayed zero remorse and he insisted on having his day in court because he wanted to prove that what had happened wasn't his fault."

"How was it *not* his fault?"

"I'm getting to that part." Jennifer looked as indignant hearing about the meeting as I had felt during it. I gestured for her to be patient. "I knew there was no way I could win on the facts. Not with a client sitting in court practically gloating over what he had done. I reported that to the senior partners and suggested they try to broker a deal with the DA for a reduction of the charges."

"And?"

"The partners wouldn't go for it. They said a plea bargain wasn't an option. It would imply guilt and, as far as we—*they* were concerned, their client was one hundred percent not guilty. The partners wanted me to prove that E. J. was provoked. That Jason goaded him into violence by coming on to him.

"E. J. turned a man's face into a Picasso painting and

carved 'fag' into his forehead because the guy smiled at him on the L, and I'm supposed to use homosexual panic as a defense? I couldn't do it. There was no way I could stand in open court, point my finger at the victim, and accuse him of something as heinous as *smiling*.

"The partners called me insubordinate and threatened to place a formal letter of reprimand in my personnel file if I didn't mount the defense they wanted. I told them they could stick their reprimands up their asses and I quit. I packed up my toys and I left. Now I've been essentially blackballed. No other firm will even take my calls, let alone consent to an interview.

"The case went to trial a couple of weeks ago. The firm trotted out its go-to guy to sit first chair. Unlike me, he did exactly what he was told. It makes him look like a homophobe, but if he makes partner, I'm sure he won't care. He can use the resulting bonus to buy a new moral compass. Closing arguments are Monday morning, so jury deliberations should begin on Monday afternoon. Then the real waiting game begins to see who gets proven right—me or the firm."

Jennifer gave me a standing ovation.

"What was that for?" I asked when she sat down again.

"There aren't many people who would choose principles over a paycheck."

"Maybe," I said, "but I miss my paycheck."

"Are you okay for money?"

"I have enough in savings to tide me over for a while. I just hate watching the balance dwindle as I transfer part of it to my checking account each month."

"Tell me something." Jennifer reached for the last bit of salad in the bowl. "Did E. J. lash out at Jason because he didn't want Jason to make a pass or because he did and he didn't want his friends to know it?"

I had asked myself the same question a dozen times—if E. J. were secretly or latently homosexual—and I had come to the same conclusion each time. "If he is gay, we don't want him on our team."

Jennifer looked at me through narrowed eyes.

"What?" I asked as I poured myself another glass of wine.

"I'm giving you a chance to change your pronoun."

"What do you mean?"

"You said 'we' again. *We* don't want him on *our* team. Was that another slip of the tongue or are you trying to tell me something?"

"Both, I guess."

"You guess?" When I reached for her empty plate, she pulled it out of my reach. "The dishes can wait." She leaned forward in her chair. "Talk to me, Sydney. What revelation did you have as a result of being on this case? Did talking to E. J. hit too close to home? Were you afraid you'd end up like he did—so filled with rage that you lashed out at anyone who showed an interest in you?"

She backed me in a corner and I came out swinging. What did I have to lose?

"I'm not E. J. I'm nothing like him. The case didn't teach me anything. *You* did. When you went to Darfur, I couldn't imagine not seeing you every day. The reality was even worse. I died a little bit more each day you were away. Each time you leave, it gets harder for me to let you go."

"Each time I come back, it gets harder for me to stay."

"Stay with me."

I reached for her hand. Once more, she pulled away.

"I told you before. One night with you wouldn't be enough for me. I need more than that."

"I can give you more than that."

She looked at me hard, her eyes examining mine. "Careful, Syd," she said. "For a minute there, I almost thought you meant that."

"I do mean it. I love you, Jen."

She shook her head. "Don't do this to me, Sydney. Don't say those words to me unless you're willing to back them up. Until you are, we don't have anything to talk about. Thanks for dinner. It was…enlightening." She pushed her chair away from the table and headed for the door.

I had finally been honest with her—with myself—and she didn't believe me. I felt my one chance at happiness slipping away, but I didn't know what to do. I didn't know how to approach her.

I had hoped that she would take my confession at face value and not question me. I had hoped that I would tell her how I felt and she would open my eyes the way I had opened my heart. That she would sweep me into the bedroom and show me what I had been missing all those years I had been hiding my feelings from her—and myself.

She opened the door but I pushed it shut before she could walk through it.

"Don't run away from this," I said. "Don't run away from me."

She rested her head against the door as if she wished she could crawl through the peephole and disappear out the other side. "We're not teenagers, Syd. I can't be with you like this and pretend it doesn't mean anything."

"Believe me, it means everything."

"What about Jack?"

"He is a mistake that I intend to rectify as soon as I can. In the meantime—"

Pressing my body against hers, I pulled her coat out of her hands and let it fall to the floor. I ran my hands through her shorn hair and kissed the back of her neck. The skin there was so soft and warm. I wanted to know what the rest felt like.

"Sydney, don't." Still facing the door, she refused to turn around.

I did a little refusing of my own. I refused to listen to her. Reaching under her—*my*—shirt, I lightly ran my fingertips over her skin. I started on her lower back and moved around to her stomach. I moved one hand up to her chest. I slid the other down the front of her jeans.

My left hand kneaded her breast. My right slipped inside her underwear, felt the coarse hairs. When my fingers found the hard knot between her legs, she gasped and sagged against me.

"Don't you want this as much as I do?" I asked.

"No, I don't." She finally faced me. "I want it more."

She kissed me and it was like high school all over again. Back then, she and I used to lock ourselves in my room and practice kissing when we were supposed to be doing our homework. I would pretend I was kissing David DiNunzio; she would pretend she was kissing Rachel Nicholson. When the marathon sessions were over, I would pretend that I didn't feel anything for her. I didn't want to go on pretending.

"Who taught you to kiss like that?" I asked breathlessly.

"You did." She leaned in to kiss me again but pulled back at the last minute. "Are you sure about this?"

"I can show you better than I can tell you." I took her hand and led her to the bedroom. The place where I slept with Jack but fantasized about her.

When I was with Jack, I reverted into the fifteen-year-old everyone had called Pizza Face. I was so self-conscious that I couldn't enjoy myself. Being with him felt like a performance. I couldn't come with him. I would come close—pardon the pun—but I had to finish the job myself after he fell asleep. I played a good game, though, so he never knew the difference. Or if he did, he never let on.

It wasn't that way with Jennifer. I wasn't frozen with her the way I was with Jack. I felt comfortable with her. Relaxed. She made me feel beautiful—supermodel gorgeous like she had promised I would one day be. I wanted her eyes on me. I wanted her hands on me. I wanted her mouth on me. One touch from her and I found what I had been searching for all my life. I learned what desire meant. How it felt.

With Jennifer, I didn't think about myself. I thought about her. About pleasing her. About what she wanted. And then I wasn't thinking. I wasn't fantasizing or pretending. I was with her. And I couldn't get enough.

"How long have you wanted this?" she asked.

I groaned as her fingers slipped inside me. My back arched against her and I pulled her closer. "Since the day I met you."

"Then what took you so long?"

"Better late than never," I said, staring into her loving eyes.

I had heard that when one woman makes love to another, the pleasure is twinned. You feel what she's doing to you, but you also feel what you're doing to her.

I knew what to do because I knew what I wanted Jennifer to do to me. I knew how to touch her because I knew how I wanted her to touch me. I knew how to kiss her because—well, because she had already shown me how.

My hands on her were hers on me. Her mouth on me was mine on her. My name on her lips was hers on mine.

The spasms began. Gently at first, then with greater and greater intensity. My initial "Oh" of surprise quickly turned into a full-throated cry. Jennifer echoed the sound.

When it was over, she said in a voice filled with awed surprise, "I can't believe we're here."

Neither could I.

"I always wanted it to happen," she said, her fingers drawing lazy circles over my bare back, "but I never thought it would."

I held her hands in mine so we could talk about the thing we had never talked about before. The thing that had kept us together and apart for over twenty years: our love for each other.

"Why didn't you ever say anything?" I asked.

"What did you want me to do, club you over the head and drag you back to my cave by your hair?"

"If you had, we could have been here a long time ago."

She shook her head. "You weren't ready."

"But I am now?"

"You've taken the first step. The question is, can you go all the way?"

I grinned at her to remind her what had just happened. "I think I just did, don't you?"

She shook her head again. "The first step was admitting it to yourself. The second step was admitting it to me. Going all the way is admitting it to everyone else. Are you ready to do that?"

I didn't respond to her question because I didn't know the answer. I wasn't eager to leave the safety—the sanctity—of my bedroom. There, we could be anyone or anything we wanted. No one could interfere. No one had to know.

I kissed her, then pressed my ear to her chest, listening to the steady beating of her heart. A heart that I would soon break. "I love you, Jen."

She kissed me on the top of my head and closed her eyes. "I love you, too, Syd. There. I said it. Better late than never, right?"

We went to sleep entwined in each other's arms and woke up the same way.

Everything looked different in the light of day. It felt different, too. I wasn't the only one who noticed.

"Any regrets?" Jennifer asked as if she expected me to respond in the affirmative.

"No," I said, wrapping her arms tighter around me.

"When are you going to tell him?"

The night before, I had been reckless and impulsive. The morning after, I was much more deliberate. I didn't want to screw anything up. Not when I was so close to getting everything I had ever wanted.

"I'll tell him tonight at dinner. Sometime between the appetizer and the main course. I don't want to hit him in the face with it when he first walks in, but I don't want him to get too comfortable or I might lose my nerve."

"I would offer to come with you, but I think I'm the last person Jack would want to see."

"You think?" I rolled over to face her. "No matter what happens, last night was the best night of my life. Never forget that. Being with you is something I've always wanted. Don't let anyone, including me, ever tell you otherwise. Deal?"

"Deal."

❖

I spent the whole afternoon planning what I would say to Jack. I would break the news to him first, then Patrick, then my parents. Jack would be hurt. He would be angry. But I felt prepared to take the barrage of abuse he would throw my way. I couldn't predict my family's reaction, but I didn't expect it to be positive.

Jack and I had reservations at Ambria. When I'd made them several weeks before, I'd had no idea then that the restaurant's romantic setting would prove to be so ironic.

I arrived first. Jack called from the hospital to let me know he was going to be late, so I treated myself to an extra glass of wine while I waited. When he arrived half an hour later, he looked like he had been put through the wringer. His eyes were red-rimmed and his hair and clothes were disheveled. When I asked him what was wrong, he said he had lost a patient. A routine procedure had gone horribly wrong with no obvious explanation why. A surgeon's worst nightmare.

It would have been incredibly callous to tell him about me and Jennifer at that moment, so I decided not to. Jack needed comfort, not additional grief. My big announcement could wait.

I broke the news to Jennifer the next day.

She gave a presentation at the hospital about the genocide in Darfur. Her words were powerful, the pictures that went along with them even more so. Many people in the audience were moved, me included. I was so proud of her. My confidante. My best friend. My lover. My all of the above.

Afterward, we met for lunch in the cafeteria. Frequent interruptions from well-wishers made talking—and eating—difficult.

"How did it go last night?" she asked, pushing away the remains of her grilled chicken sandwich. "I got worried when you didn't call. I almost drove over to your place a hundred times but I didn't want to interfere. Are you okay? How did he take it?"

I toyed with my salad, moving the wilted lettuce around my plate with my fork. "I didn't tell him."

I looked up expecting her to be surprised. To be angry. Instead, she looked disappointed. And vindicated. As if she had expected me to let her down. That was even worse. "May I ask why not?"

I told her what had happened.

"He's like you when he loses a patient," I said. "The world comes to an end until he can figure out what went wrong. I couldn't kick him when he was down. I *will* tell him but not right now."

"When?"

"I don't know. When the timing's right."

"I understand your reasons for not saying anything last night, but the longer you wait, the harder it's going to be for you to tell him. If you keep waiting for a perfect time, you're never going to find one. There's always going to be something in the way."

"Nothing has changed," I said, trying to salvage the situation. "I'm not giving up on us. I'm simply putting us on hold for a while. I still want to be with you. I just can't right now. I'm his in name only. In every other way, I'm yours. We both know that. Isn't that enough?"

"You know the answer to that question so don't ever, *ever* ask me that again." She pulled a pen and a piece of paper out of her bag and scribbled a quick note. "I'm late for a meeting with the hospital administrators. They want me to crisscross the country giving the little speech I just gave, but HR wants to know when I'll be ready to make rounds again." She looked at the note in her hands as if deciding what to do with it. Then she folded it in half and slid it toward me. "We'll talk later, okay?"

"Jen, wait."

She waved her hand to indicate that she didn't have time. She punched the Up button on the elevator and stood in front of it with her head down until the doors opened. I read her note as she waited for the other passengers to disembark.

"I won't be the lie you tell," she had written.

She boarded the elevator and I ran after her, shoving my hand between the doors before they could slide shut. I stepped inside. The doors closed behind me. I held up her note. Since we were the only ones in the car, we could talk without worrying about being overheard. I was going to ask her what her message meant, but she wouldn't let me get a word in.

"I'm not going to have an affair with you," she said, punching the button for the next floor. "I'm not emotionally equipped for that. If you're mine, be mine. You don't have to tell the whole fucking world about it, but telling your husband would be nice."

The elevator stopped on the floor that housed the neurological unit. When the doors opened, Jennifer stalked out and headed for the stairs. I trailed her. I would follow her up each of the remaining ten flights to the personnel department if I had to.

"I love you, Jen," I insisted, my voice echoing off the walls.

"That's what you keep telling me." She took the stairs two and three at a time, running—*leaping*—up them like a gazelle fleeing from a pack of hungry cheetahs.

"I never meant to hurt you."

"Or use me?"

"That's not what last night was about."

"Wasn't it?"

She turned on me. I had to pull up short to keep from running into her.

"You wanted to know why I didn't tell you how I felt?" she asked, her eyes filled with equal parts anger and hatred. "This is why. Because I knew you'd say anything to make it happen, then run away and hide after it did. Why would I tell you how much I loved you when I knew you'd do your best to make me feel ashamed of it? I'm not you, Sydney. I don't give a shit what anyone thinks. Anyone except you."

She shrugged as if that was about to change.

"But it's okay. You got what you wanted," she spat. "You got to experiment a little and that was enough for you. Now you expect things to go on being as they were. I can't pretend to be just friends with you after we—" She paused. "You know me better than that. Or at least I thought you did. You can hide from the world in your sham of a marriage if you want to, but I'm not going to help you do it. The best thing for you to do is forget last night ever happened. Forget you ever met me. I'll do the same with you. In fact, I already have."

"Jen—"

She continued up the stairs. This time, I didn't follow her.

She needed time to cool off. She needed time away from me. I gave her that time. It was the worst mistake I've ever made. I should have fought harder to get through to her. To make her hear me. To make her understand. But I let her go. I let her go and she didn't come back.

I called her and e-mailed her over and over again, but she didn't return any of my messages. The day after our aborted lunch date, she flew to the East Coast to begin her speaking tour. She made one stop—a seminar in Durham, North Carolina, at Duke University Medical School—then abruptly left the country without saying good-bye.

With no one to talk to—no one to share my feelings with—I did as she asked. I forgot about her. Her and everything and everyone else, including myself. But the memories—and the feelings that went along with them—refused to remain hidden, no matter how deeply I tried to bury them. When they returned, they brought with them a reserve of untapped strength. I found the resolve to attempt to regain what I had lost. What I had let slip through my fingers.

I had let Jennifer get away once. Twice. Never again.

She was the person I wanted to be with. And this time, I didn't care who knew it.

Chapter Eighteen

My flight to Honduras was a commercial one but it felt more like a charter. Nearly three-quarters of the seats in the small plane were filled with teenagers and their chaperones about to embark on a month-long religious mission designed to bring the native tribes in the area closer to God. When the plane skidded off the dirt runway in Tegucigalpa, I thought I was about to meet God face-to-face.

I gripped the arms of my seat with both hands as the plane slid inexorably toward the freeway. Traffic on the busy thoroughfare ground to a halt, policemen in fluorescent vests holding up progress in both directions.

"Don't worry," the passenger across the aisle from me said with a wink. "This happens every time."

"And that's supposed to make me feel better?"

"It could be worse," he said.

"How?"

"We could be those guys."

I followed his finger as he pointed out the window. Several uniformed men were jogging across the "tarmac," a narrow, rutted patch of land that looked more like a cow pasture than a runway.

"Who are they?" I asked.

"In the States, we have guys on cute little vehicles to tow planes around the concourse. In Honduras, these guys are the cute little vehicles."

As soon as we disembarked, I turned around to see if my travel companion had been pulling my leg. True to his word, though, the men lined up on both sides of the plane and pushed it back toward the terminal.

"I told you so," my new friend said. Dressed in cargo shorts, a Save The Planet T-shirt, and well-worn hiking boots, he looked like he had escaped from the pages of an adventure novel or an Abercrombie and Fitch catalog. He stuck out his hand. "Alex Matthews."

"Sydney Paulsen," I replied, using my maiden name. Though it wasn't official yet, in my mind, my days as Sydney Stanton had come to an end.

"Where are you headed?"

"Mocoron."

"Me, too. Looks like we'll be traveling together for a while longer."

A charter bus was parked a few feet away from the plane we had arrived in. A man I assumed to be the driver ticked names off his clipboard as a line of people waited to board. The people in line ranged in age from twentysomethings to obvious retirees.

As the passengers climbed the steep steps that led inside the bus, the relief driver took their bags and tossed them in the storage compartment.

I checked my watch. My bus wasn't scheduled to leave for another hour. I had hoped to use the layover to stock up on a few essentials—Hershey's with almonds, a can of coffee, and a box of Power Bars—at a shopping center in town, but it looked like my ride was leaving me.

"We've got plenty of time," Alex said as we joined the

steady stream of passengers heading from the tarmac to the crowded terminal.

He seemed to be more experienced with the way things worked in our current locale, so I took his word for it.

By the time I reached the inside of the terminal, the back of my long-sleeved T-shirt was damp with sweat. The thermometer on the side of the building read seventy-seven degrees, but the humidity made it seem much warmer. The air was so thick I could practically chew it.

The bad thing was, I knew the conditions were bound to be even worse where I was headed. Forty kilometers from the Nicaraguan border, Mocoron was on the Mosquito Coast in an area known as Central America's Little Amazon. I hoped that, unlike its Brazilian counterpart, *La Mosquitia* didn't contain frogs the size of loaves of bread or snakes as long as football fields. Okay, I might have been exaggerating about the snakes—but not by much.

I made it through Customs with no problems, always a major accomplishment in my book. Alex and I headed for the bus and took our places in line. The sun was high in the sky. If we didn't run into any delays on the road to Puerto Lempira, I felt confident we would be able to make it to Mocoron before dark. No navigable roads led into the tiny town. The primary ways to reach the underdeveloped area were by air or water— or, for the truly adventurous, on foot.

After a three-hour bus ride to Puerto Lempira, Alex and I would have to travel another hour on the Rio Mocoron before we reached our destination.

I adjusted the straps on my backpack, shifting its dead weight to a more comfortable position. I had no idea how long I planned to stay, so I had chosen items that I wouldn't mind wearing over and over again—jeans, T-shirts, canvas shorts, and a couple of sweatshirts. I had two pairs of shoes—the sandals I was wearing and the sturdy boots I would change into once I made it to camp.

Alex switched off the iPod strapped to his arm and removed the ear buds. "Is this your first trip to Honduras?"

I nodded. "Yours?"

He shook his head. "My third. It's beautiful down here, isn't it?"

I looked around at the friendly people, colorful flowers, and towering mountains that surrounded us. "Magnificent."

"That's why I keep coming back. Well, that and a certain doctor I met on my last trip. The two of us hooked up a couple of times," Alex continued, sounding like one of the housemates on *The Real World*. "We managed to stay in touch after I left—mostly through postings on each other's blogs. I'm hoping the magic will still be there when we come face-to-face again."

"What if it isn't?" I asked, wondering what I would do if I found myself in similar straits. If the animosity Jennifer felt for me the last time we saw each other was still there—or had intensified in the time since we had been apart.

"There are other fish in the sea."

How could he sound so serious about someone one second and so blasé the next? Obviously one of the perks of being young.

"What do you do in the real world?" I asked, trying to discover if he spent all his time trying to save the planet or if it were only a part-time job.

"As little as possible. What brings you to Honduras?"

"A gorgeous doctor I've known since I was three."

"Are you looking to rekindle a little magic of your own?" he asked, obviously happy that we had a common mission.

Since he had opened himself up to me, I thought he deserved the same in return. I decided to be honest with him. I had to practice on someone. Why not him? I'd probably never see him again. What could it hurt to lay everything on the line?

"If she'll have me," I said, absently rubbing the spot where my wedding ring used to rest.

"Your doctor's a she?" His green eyes twinkled, making him look like an overgrown leprechaun. "Well," he said with another wink, "mine is a he, so there you go."

Chapter Nineteen

Alex's messenger bag was crammed with dozens of magazines—some dog-eared and dated, others brand new.

When Jennifer was in Africa, I used to ship her my copies of *Sports Illustrated*, *People*, and *Entertainment Weekly* every month after I finished reading them. She and the rest of the aid workers had already pored through all of each other's books and magazines. They had heard the same CDs and watched the same DVDs so many times that they could recite each line from memory. They craved something—anything—new. Jennifer's slow but inevitable response was always an e-mailed "You made my day" in twenty-four-point type with about thirty-six exclamation points on the end. I hoped she'd feel the same way when she received her latest care package—me.

Alex shoved his hand into the recesses of the messenger bag and came out with a pack of flavored condoms. "Big night planned?" I asked as he hastily thrust the package back into the bag.

"With no running water or electricity, the *only* thing to do in Mocoron is have sex. You'll soon find that out."

I should be so lucky.

At long last, Alex retrieved a packet of chewing gum.

"Jack Daniel's is my favorite cure-all," he said. "I'm afraid this is the best I can do."

He offered the pack to me. I gratefully unwrapped a stick of Trident and popped it in my mouth. The long bus ride over rough terrain had left me feeling a little green around the gills. The boat trip wasn't doing wonders for me, either.

In Puerto Lempira, Alex and I had picked up a few supplies—a case of bottled water and nearly as much bug spray—before hitching a ride with a fisherman who rented his boat as a water taxi during the dry season. In my head, I referred to the diminutive man as Cap'n Crunch because he bore more than a passing resemblance to the picture on the cereal box.

As Cap'n Crunch navigated his battered powerboat down Rio Mocoron, Alex pulled a worn photograph out of his bag of tricks and handed it to me. Even though more than a dozen people were in the picture, I focused on only one. Jennifer, her hands on her hips and a familiar lopsided grin on her face, was in the back row. She was dressed in a T-shirt, shorts, and a sweat-stained Cubs hat. The other people in the picture were attired the same way—minus, of course, the Cubs hat.

I knew without asking that I was looking at a picture of the Mocoron clinic's medical staff. One incarnation of it, anyway. Most of the faces changed every few months or so. The version in the picture was almost a year old. Jennifer hadn't been to Mocoron since the previous spring when the mobile clinic was just getting off the ground. Now she was back and I, like Stanley looking for Livingstone, was going to find her.

Resisting the urge to caress Jennifer's image, I returned the picture. I didn't want to touch photo paper. I wanted to touch the real thing.

"That one's mine." Alex pointed to a handsome blond kneeling in the front row. "His name's Lars Johansson. He's

Swedish, which means I'll probably have to learn to love IKEA furniture, but I certainly wouldn't kick him out for eating crackers in bed. Which one's yours?"

"That one." I pointed Jennifer out to him.

"Dr. Rekowski's yours?" He seemed impressed, which pleased me.

"She *was*," I said, reminding him that I had some work to do in that regard.

"And she will be again."

I wished I could bottle his confidence. "We'll see."

Alex snapped his fingers. "I know who you are now. Dr. Rekowski used to talk about you all the time. Only she said your last name was Stanton, not Paulsen."

"It was for a while. A few things have changed since then." I thought about how far I'd come in the past few days. "Okay, a *lot* has changed since then."

My chest puffed with pride and my heart soared with hope. The way Jennifer and I had left things, I had thought she would never mention my name again—unless she were cursing me or spewing invective. Based on Alex's expression, though, whatever Jennifer had told him about me must have been positive. That meant there was still a chance for us. Her feelings couldn't have changed that much in a year, no matter what I'd done in the meantime. Or could they?

"What did she say about me?" I asked.

"What did she used to call you?" He snapped his fingers again. "The one that got away. Looks like you didn't go too far."

"Every road I take leads me right back to her. I either have a lousy sense of direction or wonderful taste in women. We'll see which one turns out to be true."

CHAPTER TWENTY

*E*stamos aquí." We're here.

The words were like music to my ears. I was so ready to see Jennifer. To stop running. To stop traveling. To stop. I had been on six plane flights in three days and I'd had no sleep the night before. I was out of gas, the fuel in my tank down to nothing but fumes.

Cap'n Crunch steered the boat toward a clearing where the rainforest met the river. He cut the engine. The boat drifted toward the shore until the hull scraped against the rich brown earth, stopping our forward momentum.

I could hear birds singing in the trees and small—at least I hoped they were small—animals moving around in the thick underbrush, but they were the only signs of life. Where was the welcoming committee?

Against my better judgment, I swung my legs over the side of the boat and jumped into the shallow water. When the rainy season began in a couple of months, the depleted river would rise by several feet, flooding some of the areas we had just floated past.

"Are we sure this is the right place?" I asked as I waded to shore.

Alex pointed to a path that had been worn into the lush

green grass. "The camp's one mile that way, give or take a few hundred yards. If this were the rainy season, the clinic would have moved to higher ground to avoid mud slides and flood waters. That location's about five miles in."

Good thing Jennifer decided to hide out in January instead of March.

I tried to convince myself that I was up to the challenge that lay ahead, but I felt like I was going to keel over at any second.

"She's worth the effort," I said under my breath. "It's only a mile. Seven minutes on the treadmill." Yeah, if the treadmill were ramped up to its highest setting and placed in a sauna.

Less than a third of the way into the hike, my legs began to feel like a pair of rubber bands that had lost their elasticity. My lungs burned as if I were running a marathon. Sweat soaked my clothes, adding a good five pounds to the load I was already carrying. Mosquitoes the size of bats threatened to carry me away. The area we were in was called the Mosquito Coast because of the native Miskito tribe that called it home, but you could have fooled me.

Alex led the way, the case of bottled water perched on his shoulder. We had bought the water for the clinic's staff and their patients. With no source of water onsite, they had to haul buckets of the precious liquid from the river and boil it for hours in order to make it safe for drinking. I was tempted—not for the first time—to take one of the bottles for myself. I refrained, telling myself I could hold out for ten more minutes.

"Okay back there?" he asked when he finally noticed that the gap between the two of us had grown from a couple of feet to nearly ten.

I was desperate to see Jennifer but I had pushed myself to the limit. I needed a break.

"Give me a minute to catch my breath and I'll be as right as rain."

I took off my backpack and looked for a place to sit down. My head was spinning and my heart was beating much too fast. My brain was in a fog, my thoughts muddled and confused. I felt the way I had in O'Hare on Tuesday when, stressed over Jennifer's absence and the Subway Slasher case's omnipresence, I had rushed to catch a plane and lost myself on the way.

No, I thought, *this can't be happening again.*

I shook my head to try to clear it. Then the rubber band snapped. The sky tilted crazily and the ground rushed up to meet my back. My eyelids slid shut and I was powerless to stop them.

Chapter Twenty-one

Something cold and wet lay on my forehead. Something cold and metallic sliced at my T-shirt. A hand slapped my left cheek hard enough to sting. I groaned as something hard rubbed painfully across my breastbone.

"Come on, Sleeping Beauty. Wake up."

Fingers pried open my right eyelid. A small round light waved back and forth, blinding me with its brightness.

I squeezed my eyes shut, groaned again, and tried to turn away. I tried to sit up.

"Not so fast."

Strong hands grabbed me by my shoulders and forced me back down. My stomach lurched at the sudden movement. I swung wildly at the hands that sought to restrain me.

"I will tie you down if I have to, Syd, so don't try me."

The authoritative voice was as familiar to me as my own. "Jennifer?"

I opened my eyes and her face filled my vision. She looked worried. About me? So she did care.

"There you are," she whispered as her thumb caressed my cheek. "Welcome back to the land of the living."

Her touch was gentle, her voice soothing. I closed my eyes again, wanting her to sing me to sleep.

"No," she chided, smacking me in the face again. "Stay with me."

I opened my eyes again. "Stop hitting me," I said, my voice raspy.

"I will if you stay awake long enough for me to examine you."

When she hit me again, I hit her back.

"What was that for?" she asked, rubbing her arm.

"You were enjoying it too much."

We were in a large canvas tent, military issue from the size of it. Boxes of medical supplies lined one wall, boxes of canned goods another. Outside, a gas-powered generator coughed and spluttered to life. The thick exhaust it emitted made my nausea even worse. Several people crowded in the tent's open doorway, cutting off my access to fresh air.

"Is she all right?" Alex asked.

"That's what I'm about to find out," Jennifer replied. "Thanks again for getting her here. I owe you a beer—or twelve. Now I need some privacy so I can examine her. Give us some room, okay, guys?"

A little girl stood in front of the group. She had copper-colored skin, short black hair, and the biggest, brownest eyes I had ever seen. The soccer ball in her arms was almost bigger than she was. Perched on her head, cinched as tight as its adjustable strap would allow, was Jennifer's prize possession, her Cubs hat. I could see the faint remnants of Greg Maddux's and Ryne Sandberg's signatures on the bill.

"See you tomorrow, Dr. Jen?" the little girl asked in heavily accented English.

"Sure thing," Jennifer said with a broad smile. "I'll bet you won't score on me tomorrow, though."

The little girl's eyes sparkled at the challenge. "I bet I will. I can bend it like Beckham."

Alex and the rest of the adults ushered everyone out, leaving me and Jennifer alone.

Jennifer closed the tent flap and returned to the stainless steel table where I lay. She regarded me before beginning her examination. I didn't know how I looked, but if I looked as good as I felt, I looked like shit. It wasn't how I wanted our reunion to kick off, that's for sure.

"Do you know where you are?" she asked as she pulled on a pair of latex gloves.

"It looks like I'm in the middle of nowhere, but I hope I'm in Mocoron. If I'm not, this will have to do because I am *not* getting on another plane, boat, or bus today."

Jennifer blew on the metal part of her stethoscope to warm it. She pressed the stethoscope against my chest and listened to my heart. "I always knew you were crazy. You didn't have to prove it to me. Deep breath in." She moved the stethoscope to my back. "Again."

I obliged as best I could. I felt as if I had a boulder sitting on my chest.

"You owe me a T-shirt," I said. The one I had been wearing lay in tatters on the floor.

"In order for me to be able to rule out the possibility of an allergic reaction, I had to check your skin for insect bites. The shirt was collateral damage."

I lifted one foot, then the other as Jennifer removed my boots and dropped them on the floor. My wet socks soon joined them.

"But I loved that shirt," I whined. "We bought it at the Bruce Springsteen concert at Soldier Field. Remember how we camped out for a week outside the stadium to get tickets because they weren't available online?"

Jennifer stopped examining my feet and put her hands on her hips.

"Sydney, I'll buy you another shirt. I'll even get Springsteen to sign it for you. Are you happy now?"

"I'm getting there."

I had gotten a rise out of her. I had penetrated the professional demeanor she was using as armor and, for a split second, she had treated me like her friend, not her patient. It wasn't much, but it was a start.

"Does anyone know where you are?" she asked as she resumed her inspection. Her hands slid up my legs, looking for—I assumed—breaks in the skin or little creatures that had decided to hitch a ride.

"Everyone does. They also know why I'm here."

Her eyes flicked toward my face, then she looked away. "Why *are* you here?"

"Because anywhere you are, that's where I want to be."

The silence stretched on for several seconds as I waited in vain for her to respond to what I had said.

"You let someone score on you?" I asked, soldiering on by changing the subject. "You used to be a much better goalie than that." She still held school records—both high school and college—for most career shutouts.

"I used to be much better at a lot of things. Judging a person's character, for example." She wrapped a blood pressure cuff around my left arm and slid the stethoscope underneath it while the cuff inflated.

I always panicked when I got my blood pressure checked. I had an irrational fear that the cuff would malfunction, growing tighter and tighter until, finally, it ripped off my arm.

Jennifer frowned when she saw the reading. "Your blood pressure's low; your pulse is rapid—"

"That's from seeing you," I said. She didn't laugh at the joke, stretching my already-frayed nerves nearly to their breaking point. "Could I have a Tic Tac or something? My mouth tastes like a cow crawled in it and died."

Refusing to be distracted, she stuck a thermometer in my mouth to shut me up. Then she shined her pen light into my eyes again. "Your pupils are dilated and your skin is clammy," she said, continuing her clinical recitation of my symptoms. I flinched when she pinched the skin on my forearm. "When is the last time you had something to drink?"

I pressed down on the thermometer with my tongue to keep it from falling out of my mouth. "Yesterday, I think."

"Thought so." She pressed a cold bottle of Gatorade into my hand, then took the thermometer out of my mouth and checked the reading. "Your temperature's slightly elevated, but it isn't high enough to worry about. I'll check it again in an hour to be sure."

She tossed me a box of breath mints. I let three of them slide into my mouth while she jotted some notes on my chart.

"What's the verdict, Doc?"

She lifted the bottle of Gatorade toward my mouth, reminding me to drink. "As I suspected, you're dehydrated, but you'll be fine. I'm going to give you some fluids. Between the IV and the Gatorade, you should be up and around in no time. Lie down." She said it so forcefully I wished we were in bed instead of an examination room.

After disinfecting the inside of my left arm with an alcohol wipe, she reached into a cabinet behind the examination table, pulled out a bag of glucose, and prepared an IV drip. Not fond of needles, I turned away when she headed toward me with one big enough to euthanize a horse. She thumped a vein in the crook of my elbow until it rose up in protest. Then she slid the IV in and taped it in place.

"This should take about an hour, so make yourself

comfortable." She took the half-empty bottle of Gatorade from me and drank the rest of it in one long swallow. "Now you can try to get some sleep. I'm sure you need it. If you have trouble nodding off, there's a five-year-old copy of *Ladies' Home Journal* floating around here somewhere. It should put you right out."

She dropped her gloves and the empty bottle in the trash and turned to leave.

"Your bedside manner could use a little work," I told her retreating form. She stopped but didn't turn around. "I'll bet that's something you've never heard before." She picked up stride again. "I know you love me so don't act like you don't." Another pause. "If you didn't care, you wouldn't have sounded so frightened when you couldn't get me to regain consciousness."

"You're my patient. You're entitled to the highest possible standard of care."

She sounded so serious I almost believed her. Then I saw the small smile tugging at the corners of her mouth. Still, I wasn't quite forgiven. She made that clear when she pulled up a chair and sat next to my makeshift bed.

"I won't deny that I love you," she said after heaving a heavy sigh. "I couldn't do that if I tried. And, believe me, I've tried. My life would be so much easier if I'd never met you. Unfortunately, it also wouldn't be nearly as rich."

I could feel her hesitate.

"But?" I prompted.

"I don't know if I can trust you. How do I know you won't run away and hide the first time our relationship stops being fun and begins to feel like work?"

"You mean like you did?"

She tilted her head as if she didn't know what I was talking about. I gladly filled her in.

"You're blaming me for the distance between us, but this time it's not my fault. You're the one who ran and hid, not me. I told Jack just like I said I would. Yes, you were right. There was no perfect time. Yes, it hurt and, yes, I felt terrible doing it, but I did it."

I held up my left hand so she could see that I wasn't wearing my wedding ring.

"I left him, Jen. I'm free."

I expected some kind of reaction from her, but she didn't give me anything. Undaunted, I kept going.

"The way I feel about you is out in the open now. Everyone knows."

"Who's everyone?" She leaned back, moving farther away from me when what I wanted was for her to move closer.

"Jack, Mom, Dad, Patrick, Kristin, and, since the only secrets Marcus has ever been able to keep are yours, probably half of Chicago by now. Everyone I know knows that I'm a lesbian and it doesn't matter. It doesn't matter to me or to them. What matters is you can't bring yourself to trust me. Yes, I hurt you once. More than once. But you hurt me, too. You kept telling me all the reasons you couldn't fall for me—straight, married, best friend—but you never told me any of the reasons you could. If you had given me some encouragement—if we had talked to each other instead of hiding from our feelings—"

She extended her hand as if she meant to shake hands.

"What?" I asked.

"Just take my hand." When I did as she asked, she introduced herself as if we were meeting for the first time. "Hi, I'm Jennifer Rekowski. You are?"

"Sydney," I replied, feeling patently silly.

"Do you have a last name, Sydney?"

"Paulsen."

"It's a pleasure to meet you, Sydney Paulsen." She shook my hand and didn't let go. "Are you seeing anyone?"

"I'm not sure. I'd like to be." She let go of my hand, putting me on the defensive. The best defense is a good offense, so I brought out my big guns. "I love you, Jen, and I want to spend the rest of my life proving it to you. I don't trek through the rainforest for just anyone, you know."

"Technically, you didn't trek. You were carried."

"Details."

As I looked into her eyes, I thought I saw the ice begin to melt. Instead of going through the wall she had erected, I tried to go around it.

"What would you have me do?" I asked. "What penance would you have me pay? Tell me and I'll do it. As long as it means that when I've paid it, you and I will be okay. I love you, Jen. You know that as well as I do. I can't promise you that life with me will be perfect. I can't promise you that there won't be subjects on which we agree to disagree, but I can promise you that I will never again deny who I am and what you mean to me. Think about it. Do you honestly believe that I'd come all this way just to blow smoke up your ass?"

She smiled. "I wouldn't put it past you. If I remember correctly, you once drove five hundred miles just to short sheet my bed."

"Well, that was different. You shouldn't have prank called me at three in the morning."

"Should I have waited until four?" We laughed into each other's eyes for a moment and I felt our once-tenuous bond regain strength. "God," she said, burying her hands in her hair as if she wanted to pull it out by the roots, "what am I going to do with you?"

"Love me?" I asked.

"I already do." I held out my hand to her. The one without

the IV attached to it. She kissed the back of my hand and held it in both of hers. "What do you want? The house in the suburbs with the white picket fence and the two-car garage? I can't give that to you. Not from here. And I can't not be here. Or places like it. I love this work. This is what I do. I would go crazy if I opened a cushy private practice on Lakeshore Drive and sat around twiddling my thumbs all day. I'm not built that way."

"I want your face to be the first thing I see in the morning and the last thing I see at night. Whether that's in Chicago or here, that's enough for me. I know how much being here means to you. I wouldn't dare ask you not to come. Not as long as I can come with you."

Her eyes widened as if she had never received a similar offer. "Do you mean that?"

"I'm here now, aren't I? Overlooking, of course, the fact that I'm flat on my back at the moment."

She caressed my cheek. "You'll be up and around in no time. You've got the best doctor in Honduras taking care of you." She took her hand away. "But I can't ask you to stay here. The generator's on its last legs, the well's falling apart—"

I held up a hand to stop her.

"You're not asking. I'm offering. It was my idea, remember? Don't you dare ask me to leave."

"I wouldn't dream of it." She, more than anyone, knew how stubborn I could be. "Where do you see yourself in five years?"

Even though the question came out of the blue, I didn't need time to formulate a response.

"Living with you in an apartment in Andersonville with one hyperactive boxer and maybe a cat or two to even things out. You've been offered tenure at the hospital. You accept it on the condition that you can spend half the year volunteering—

three months in the field, three in the women's clinic you've helped establish. I'm practicing law again. On my own terms this time, not someone else's. You and I host family dinners once a week. Everyone comes—Mom, Dad, Patrick and Kristin and the boys, your parents, Marcus, Trevor, and all our friends. Life is good."

"Sounds like you've thought this out," she said, her eyes warm and inviting.

"Not really," I teased her. "Do you like my vision of the future or would you rather change it?"

I expected her to call me on the carpet for my presumptuousness, but she didn't.

"Syd," she said, welcoming me back into her arms as well as her heart, "I wouldn't change a thing."

Chapter Twenty-two

I was in the middle of the ocean when it happened.
     I was drifting aimlessly with the tide when I realized that I didn't know where the past two years had gone. So much had happened—and so fast—that I hadn't been able to keep up.

Jennifer and I had moved in together well ahead of our five-year plan. Two months after I had tracked her down in order to beg her forgiveness, we had returned to Chicago and gone apartment hunting. After three weeks of looking, we had been able to move her out of the apartment she shared with Marcus and into a gorgeous two-story townhouse in Andersonville, one of Chicago's historic (and most Sapphic) neighborhoods. The same day we had closed on the apartment, I had inked another contract—one that had made me a member of the district attorney's office. It's hard work, but a job I enjoy immensely.

When our friends had discovered that Jennifer and I were an item, we had been inundated not with "I told you so" but "What took you so long?"

Even Natalie had said she was happy for us. When she told us she was glad we had finally found each other, I believed she actually meant it. Thankfully, Jack had been able to move on as well.

He hadn't offered any resistance when I initiated divorce proceedings. In fact, he had even wished me well. It sounds strange to say, but the two of us are much better friends now than we were at any point of our romantic relationship. He had begun dating one of the psych counselors at the hospital about four months after our divorce was final. They had run off to Las Vegas one weekend and gotten married in a drive-through chapel owned and operated by an Elvis impersonator (skinny Elvis, not fat Elvis). Surprisingly, they're still together. Our paths don't often cross, but I hear they're happy.

Good for him. He wasn't a bad guy. He simply wasn't the right person for me.

Shortly after I had become a free woman, my parents had moved to a retirement community in Mesa, Arizona, picking a spot just a stone's throw from the Cubs' spring training facilities. After hearing Mom and Dad wax rhapsodic about the city, the climate, and the great seats at the spring training games (yeah, that and a cable package that included WGN was what had sold my father on the idea in the first place), Jennifer's parents had followed suit a few months later.

That Christmas had been special in more ways than one. Besides being my first Christmas with Jennifer—and the first time our parents had been home since they'd moved—it was also when my niece Kelly had decided to make her grand entrance. With just a look, the cute little seven-pounder had brought her father to his knees.

"I've got a daughter," Patrick had said, tears streaming down his face as he'd held his third child for the first time. "Syd, I don't know what I'm supposed to do."

"Neither do I," I'd said, admiring the new addition to our family while Jennifer babysat my nephews and our parents visited with a game but tired Kristin, "but I'm sure we'll figure it out together."

A loud splash off to my right brought me back to the present. Jennifer, as graceful as a dolphin and about as playful as one, swam toward me. "It's going to be another hour before lunch," she said, knuckling saltwater out of her eyes.

I looked over at *The Painted Lady*. Anchored twenty feet away, her deck was empty except for Ali, the boxer Jennifer bought me for my birthday last year. (We haven't gotten around to picking out the cats yet. One step at a time.) Seeing me, thirteen-month-old Ali barked and wagged her stubby little tail as if to say, "What are you doing bobbing around out there when you could be playing with me?" I waved to her to acknowledge her greeting.

"What's the hold up?" I asked Jennifer.

"Our gracious hostesses got a little distracted while they were making the *empanadas*."

Marcy and Ana had gotten back together after I left Key West. Leaving without saying good-bye and "I'm sorry" wasn't my proudest moment. Marcy deserved better. Despite all that, I like to think that I had a hand in her and Ana's happiness.

Jennifer and I visited them a couple of weeks a year, recharging our batteries while we renewed our friendships.

The first time she had met Marcy, Jennifer had turned to me and said in a voice so low only I could hear it, "You were right. She *does* have great legs."

"It's okay," I had said. "Yours are the only ones I want wrapped around me."

"They'd better be."

Ana and Jennifer had bonded right away, erasing my fears that there would be tension between them because of the potential love triangle (square?) I had nearly placed us in when I was finding my way back to myself. As for me and Marcy, we had picked up right where we had left off—minus the whole wanting to get into each other's pants thing. We reserved those feelings exclusively for Jennifer and Ana.

"If the boat's rocking, don't bother knocking," Jennifer said.

"Sounds like a great idea, don't you think?"

"What are you suggesting?"

"What do you think?" I swam over to her and wrapped my legs around her waist. Our relationship was incredible. I couldn't get enough of her. In and out of bed. Thankfully, she felt the same way. I licked the side of her neck. "What do you say? Are you up for a little afternoon delight?"

Under the water, Jennifer cupped her hands under my hips. "Make me an offer."

I suggested a race back to the boat.

"If I win, you have to put on that sexy little teddy you didn't think I saw you slip in your suitcase when we packed to come down here."

"And if I win?"

I sucked her left earlobe into my mouth and felt her shudder. "If you win, I won't wear anything at all."

"You're on."

We moved into starting position.

"We go on three," I said. "One. Two."

Jennifer began to head for the boat on two-and-a-half. Her kicking calves stirred up nearly as much white water as an outboard motor.

"Cheater!" I called out. Ali's high-pitched bark seconded my motion.

"You look much better in your birthday suit than I do in my teddy," Jennifer yelled over her shoulder as she extended her lead.

I couldn't wait to compare the two.

I dug through the water, chasing after the woman I loved in the place I had learned the most important lesson in my life: sometimes you have to forget who you were to remember who you are.

About the Author

Yolanda Wallace is not a professional writer, but she plays one in her spare time. She has written dozens of short stories, which have appeared in multiple anthologies including *UniformSex*, *Body Check*, *Bedroom Eyes*, *Best Lesbian Love Stories: New York City*, and *Best Lesbian Love Stories: Summer Flings*. *In Medias Res* is Yolanda's first published novel. She and her partner of eight years live in beautiful coastal Georgia. They are parents to four children of the four-legged variety—a four-year-old boxer and three cats ranging in age from five to eight. A writer since childhood, Yolanda has also become an avid photographer. She can often be found wandering the world trying to capture on film the elusive images she sees in her head.

Books Available From Bold Strokes Books

The Midnight Hunt by L.L. Raand. Medic Drake McKennan takes a chance and loses, and her life will never be the same—because when she wakes up after surviving a life-threatening illness, she is no longer human. (978-1-60282-140-8)

Long Shot by D. Jackson Leigh. Love isn't safe, which is exactly why equine veterinarian Tory Greyson wants no part of it—until Leah Montgomery and a horse that won't give up convince her otherwise. (978-1-60282-141-5)

In Medias Res by Yolanda Wallace. Sydney has forgotten her entire life, and the one woman who holds the key to her memory, and her heart, doesn't want to be found. (978-1-60282-142-2)

Awakening to Sunlight by Lindsey Stone. Neither Judith or Lizzy is looking for companionship, and certainly not love—but when their lives become entangled, they discover both. (978-1-60282-143-9)

Fever by VK Powell. Hired gun Zakaria Chambers is hired to provide a simple escort service to philanthropist Sara Ambrosini, but nothing is as simple as it seems, especially love. (978-1-60282-135-4)

High Risk by JLee Meyer. Can actress Kate Hoffman really risk all she's worked for to take a chance on love? Or is it already too late? (978-1-60282-136-1)

Missing Lynx by Kim Baldwin and Xenia Alexiou. On the trail of a notorious serial killer, Elite Operative Lynx's growing attraction to a mysterious mercenary could be her path to love—or to death. (978-1-60282-137-8)

Spanking New by Clifford Henderson. A poignant, hilarious, unforgettable look at life, love, gender, and the essence of what makes us who we are. (978-1-60282-138-5)

Magic of the Heart by C.J. Harte. CEO Susan Hettinger and wild, impulsive rock star M.J. Carson couldn't be more different if they tried—but opposites attract in ways neither woman can resist. (978-1-60282-131-6)

Ambereye by Gill McKnight. Jolie Garoul is falling in love with her assistant. The big problem is, Jolie is a werewolf. (978-1-60282-132-3)

Collision Course by C.P. Rowlands. Tragedy leaves Brie O'Malley and Jordan Carter fearful and alone. Can they find the courage to take a second chance on love? (978-1-60282-133-0)

Mephisto Aria by Justine Saracen. Opera singer Katherina Marov's destiny may be to repeat the mistakes of her father when she becomes involved in a dangerous love affair. (978-1-60282-134-7)

Battle Scars by Meghan O'Brien. Returning Iraq war veteran Ray McKenna struggles with the battle scars that can only be healed by love. (978-1-60282-129-3)

Chaps by Jove Belle. Eden Metcalf wants nothing more than to flee from her troubled past and travel the open road—until she runs into rancher Brandi Cornwell. (978-1-60282-127-9)

Lightbearer by John Caruso. Lucifer dares to question the premise of creation itself and reveals that sin may be all that stands between us and living hell. (978-1-60282-130-9)

The Seeker by Ronica Black. FBI profiler Kennedy Scott battles ghosts from her past, deadly obsession, and the evil that haunts her. (978-1-60282-128-6)

Power Play by Julie Cannon. Businesswomen Tate Monroe and Victoria Sosa are at odds in the boardroom, but not in the bedroom. (978-1-60282-125-5)

The Remarkable Journey of Miss Tranby Quirke by Elizabeth Ridley. When love enters Tranby's life in the form of a beautiful nineteen-year-old student, Lysette McDonald, she embarks on the most remarkable journey of all. (978-1-60282-126-2)

Returning Tides by Radclyffe. Insurance investigator Ashley Walker faces more than a dangerous opponent when she returns to the town, and the woman, she left behind. (978-1-60282-123-1)

Veritas by Anne Laughlin. When the hallowed halls of academia become the stage for murder, newly appointed Dean Beth Ellis's search for the truth leads her to unexpected discoveries about her own heart. (978-1-60282-124-8)

The Pleasure Planner by Larkin Rose. Pleasure purveyor Bree Hendricks treats love like a commodity until Logan Delaney makes Bree the client in her own game. (978-1-60282-121-7)

everafter by Nell Stark and Trinity Tam. Valentine Darrow is bitten by a vampire on her way to propose to her lover Alexa Newland, and their lives and love are placed in mortal jeopardy. (978-1-60282-119-4)

Summer Winds by Andrews & Austin. When Maggie Turner hires a ranch hand to help work her thousand acres, she never expects to be attracted to the very young, very female Cash Tate. (978-1-60282-120-0)

Beggar of Love by Lee Lynch. Jefferson is the lover every woman wants to be—or to have. A revealing saga of lesbian sexuality. (978-1-60282-122-4)

The Seduction of Moxie by Colette Moody. When 1930s Broadway actress Violet London meets speakeasy singer Moxie Valette, she is instantly attracted and her Hollywood trip takes an unexpected turn. (978-1-60282-114-9)

Goldenseal by Gill McKnight. When Amy Fortune returns to her childhood home, she discovers something sinister in the air—but is former lover Leone Garoul stalking her or protecting her? (978-1-60282-115-6)

Romantic Interludes 2: Secrets edited by Radclyffe and Stacia Seaman. An anthology of sensual lesbian love stories: passion, surprises, and secret desires. (978-1-60282-116-3)

Femme Noir by Clara Nipper. Nora Delaney meets her match in Max Abbott, a sex-crazed dame who may or may not have the information Nora needs to solve a murder—but can she contain her lust for Max long enough to find out? (978-1-60282-117-0)

The Reluctant Daughter by Lesléa Newman. Heartwarming, heartbreaking, and ultimately triumphant—the story every daughter recognizes of the lifelong struggle for our mothers to really see us. (978-1-60282-118-7)

Erosistible by Gill McKnight. When Win Martin arrives at a luxurious Greek hotel for a much-anticipated week of sun and sex with her new girlfriend, she is stunned to find her ex-girlfriend, Benny, is the proprietor. Aeros Ebook. (978-1-60282-134-7)

Looking Glass Lives by Felice Picano. Cousins Roger and Alistair become lifelong friends and discover their sexuality amidst the backdrop of twentieth-century gay culture. (978-1-60282-089-0)

Breaking the Ice by Kim Baldwin. Nothing is easy about life above the Arctic Circle—except, perhaps, falling in love. At least that's what pilot Bryson Faulkner hopes when she meets Karla Edwards. (978-1-60282-087-6)

It Should Be a Crime by Carsen Taite. Two women fulfill their mutual desire with a night of passion, neither expecting more until law professor Morgan Bradley and student Parker Casey meet again…in the classroom. (978-1-60282-086-9)

Rough Trade edited by Todd Gregory. Top male erotica writers pen their own hot, sexy versions of the term "rough trade," producing some of the hottest, nastiest, and most dangerous fiction ever published. (978-1-60282-092-0)

The High Priest and the Idol by Jane Fletcher. Jemeryl and Tevi's relationship is put to the test when the Guardian sends Jemeryl on a mission that puts her not only in harm's way, but back into the sights of a previous lover. (978-1-60282-085-2)

Point of Ignition by Erin Dutton. Amid a blaze that threatens to consume them both, firefighter Kate Chambers and property owner Alexi Clark redefine love and trust. (978-1-60282-084-5)

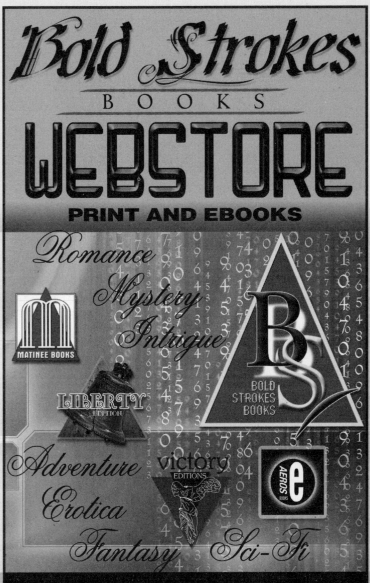